W9-BSX-215

CITY OF KAWARTHA LAKES

JAN -- 2016

TREASURE FREIGHT

OTHER FIVE STAR WESTERNS
BY PETER DAWSON:

Treasure Freight

A WESTERN SEXTET

Peter Dawson

FIVE STAR

A part of Gale, Cengage Learning

GALE
CENGAGE Learning

Farmington Hills, Mich • San Francisco • New York • Waterville, Maine
Meriden, Conn • Mason, Ohio • Chicago

GALE
CENGAGE Learning·

LIBRARY OF CONGRESS CATALOGING-IN-PUBLICATION DATA

Dawson, Peter, 1907–1957.
  [Short stories. Selections]
  Treasure freight : a western sextet / Peter Dawson. — First edition.
      pages ; cm
      ISBN 978-1-4328-2855-4 (hardcover) — ISBN 1-4328-2855-X (hardcover)
      I. Dawson, Peter, 1907–1957. Boomerang bounty. II. Title.
  PS3507.A848A6 2015
  813'.52—dc23   2014038262

First Edition. First Printing: February 2015.
Published in conjunction with Golden West Literary Agency.
Find us on Facebook– https://www.facebook.com/FiveStarCengage
Visit our website– http://www.gale.cengage.com/fivestar/
Contact Five Star™ Publishing at FiveStar@cengage.com

Printed in the United States of America
1 2 3 4 5 6 7 19 18 17 16 15

ADDITIONAL COPYRIGHT INFORMATION

5

CONTENTS

* * * * *

BOOMERANG BOUNTY

* * * * *

The author's original title for this story was "Boomerang Bounty". The story was submitted to Mike Tilden at Popular Publications on April 3, 1937 and he bought it for *Star Western*. Peter Dawson was paid $90.00. The title was changed to "No More Towns to Tame" when it appeared in the issue dated August, 1937. It was first collected in the anthology *Star Western* (Gramercy, 1995) edited by Jon Tuska under the author's original title, and it now is collected here under that title.

I

He was medium tall and thin, and his eyes were a cold gray, deep-set in a lean, bronzed face. He wore a black Stetson, a dark gray vest over a gray shirt, waist overalls tucked into soft high-heeled boots. His guns were a pair of horn-handled, silver-mounted Colt .38s riding low in open holsters at his thighs. Chiefly it was the eyes and the guns that you noticed.

From across the cow-town street a cowpuncher and a girl watched him dismount and throw the reins of his sleek, straight-legged dun stallion over the tie rail in front of the bank.

"Who is he, Ed?" the girl asked.

She was too far away to see the stranger's eyes, but she had caught the white reflected sun-glint from his weapons. That, plus her long familiarity with this country, made the presence disturbing. She was frowning as she gazed up at her companion, but, even with the frown, a softness touched her glance that heightened her good looks and made it at once obvious that this was the man of her choice.

"I wouldn't know," Ed answered. "But I'd like to have the hardware he's packing. It'd pay up a good share of the interest on my note this fall." He was well set up, broad-shouldered and tall. Even a close observer would have overlooked the shabbiness of his outfit, for it was clean and fit him well.

No one in the bank knew the stranger. But they all saw him enter, and, when he sauntered back and asked the teller in the last cage if he might speak to Tade Wardow, the president, he

11

was given the respectful answer: "Yes, sir. I'll call him."

"Never mind. I'll do the calling."

Before the teller could protest, the stranger had walked around the end of the counter and was crossing to the glass-paneled door that was lettered *President*.

He didn't knock at the door; he pushed it open, and stood looking in as it swung back. Tade Wardow glanced up from where he sat behind his polished mahogany desk. A belligerent frown gathered on his round plump face: "I'm busy," he snapped. "You'll have to wait outside."

"I'm Lonesome Barkley," the stranger drawled in soft tones that were meant only for Wardow's ears.

His words seemed to put sudden fear into the banker's steel-blue eyes. With an attempt at affability, Wardow managed to get out: "Come in. Come in, and take a chair."

The stranger stepped in and let the door swing shut behind him. But he made no move toward the chair Wardow indicated. Instead, he leaned indolently against the wall and hooked his thumbs in his belt.

"Talk, Wardow," he said.

Tade Wardow's manner now was somehow ridiculous compared to his blunt arrogance of a moment ago. He opened his mouth to speak, closed it again, and swallowed with difficulty—as though his mouth was full of cotton. He was a big man, young, dark, and handsome in a well-fed way. His black coat and spotlessly clean white shirt fit his thick chest and shoulders faultlessly.

The banker's glance dropped down to take in the stranger's guns. Finally he got out: "Don't be proddy, Lonesome. No one else knows."

"Go on."

"It's like I said in my letter," Wardow explained hastily. "I'm the only one Jim Hogan talked to. He sent for me before he died. We were alone. I'm the only one who knows about it."

"What?"

"About . . . about. . . ." The banker was having difficulty with his throat just then.

"About the stage robbery up at Tentpole?" Lonesome prompted.

Wardow nodded stiffly. "That's it."

"All right. You know that Jim and I did it."

"Get this straight, Lonesome. I wouldn't go to the law with what I know. I'd. . . ."

"You'd know better."

The words were soft-spoken, spaced deliberately, but Wardow cringed visibly at the threat of them. Lonesome laughed softly, unpleasantly, seeing the banker shrink down into his chair. His two blunt hands clutched the chair arms until the skin on his knuckles showed a dead white.

"I swear to God I wouldn't," Wardow breathed hoarsely. "I brought you down here for something else . . . something with money in it."

"I'm still listening."

"There's a mine payroll due here this afternoon," Wardow said. "It's to be stored in this vault overnight . . . eleven thousand dollars. It's covered by insurance . . . if . . . if anything should happen to it."

Lonesome Barkley's expression altered imperceptibly as he listened; his lean features hardened, and two bright red spots crept in under the tan of his skin, high up on his cheekbones. Seeing it, a doctor would have suspected that Lonesome was a sick man and that something beyond a violent inner emotion caused that heightening of color. Wardow was no doctor and, besides, he was too blind with fear to notice. But he could have had his warning then of what was coming.

"It's a perfect layout," the banker went on, heartened by

Lonesome's silence. "I'll give you the combination to the vault and you can do the job tonight. There won't be any risk." He leaned back from his desk and reached down into a drawer at his side.

As he moved, Lonesome shoved out from the wall. Seeing this and understanding it, Wardow added hastily: "It's not a gun, Lonesome. Only the combination. I've written it down."

He extended his hand and opened it. A small white card lay in his palm, with two lines of numbers written on it in a neatly penciled hand. On the card lay a plain six-pointed spur rowel.

"What's that?" Lonesome asked.

"The rowel?" Wardow shrugged. "I want this left in the vault after you do the job."

Lonesome came over to the desk and picked the steel crescent off Wardow's green blotter. He looked at it, then at Wardow, and asked quietly: "A frame-up?"

"You can call it that."

Lonesome waited until the silence lengthened awkwardly. "So you think I can handle it?"

A measure of the banker's confidence returned. He shrugged his sloping shoulders carelessly in answer, saying: "Why not? Who'd ever suspect Lonesome Jim Barkley, the famous hell-town marshal?" He chuckled and a look of admiration crept into the glance he focused on his visitor. "You've been slick, Lonesome, according to what Jim Hogan told me. First it was that Tentpole job with Jim siding you. Then you went on alone to Benson, then Granite City. Maybe that's why they call you Lonesome."

"Maybe it is."

"You did a good job taming those towns, made your name with guns while you wore a marshal's badge. It's none of my business what else besides law-making you did in those places."

The color on Lonesome's cheeks heightened. "Supposing I

told you that the Tentpole job was the only one, Wardow?"

"Supposing you did? If that's your story, stick to it. Your secret's safe with. . . ."

The flashing downswing of Lonesome's right arm clipped off the words. Tade Wardow lunged up out of his chair, his eyes dilated in stark horror as Lonesome swiveled up the blunt snout of his .38. The weapon rose and fell in a swift chopping stroke that caught the banker high above the right temple. The blow drove him to his knees, so that his solid bulk hit the carpeted floor with a jarring thud. He fell backward, knocking the chair aside, then lay there without moving.

Lonesome Barkley stared down at the inert figure for five seconds; he was breathing hard from the exertion, with a rising flush mounting to his face. All at once he put a hand to his mouth and coughed; it was a deep, hollow-chested rattle that made him stoop over in pain. He coughed again, and again the spasm of pain doubled him up. Half a minute later he straightened once more, drew a deep breath, and the tide of color gradually receded from his face.

He wasn't thinking of Wardow then; he was remembering Harry Quinn, the tinhorn gambler in the saloon up in Granite City who had cashed in with a cough like his own. Harry had looked more like a mummy than a man who had lived and breathed and bet his roll on the turn of a card.

Lonesome hadn't been to a doctor about his lungs; he was afraid to hear the truth. Now, as always when these coughing fits hit him, he was wondering how much longer he had; it might take years, like it had with Quinn, or it might be over in a few short months.

He looked down at Wardow dispassionately, knowing this breed of man and hating it. Not many had earned Lonesome Barkley's hatred and lived; some had met a swift and violent death in facing the lead slugs of his .38s; a few had known the man they faced and ridden out of his life. Jim Hogan was one of the latter.

So Jim had talked. And, as a result, the one dishonest act of Lonesome's life was striking back at him. He should have killed Hogan that night on the road near Tentpole, killed him instead of losing his head and cutting down on the stage driver. That was years ago, when Lonesome's youthful pride had turned more to demonstrating his uncanny swiftness with a gun than to realizing what would come out of the unbridled use of it.

Hogan's dare that night had made Lonesome side him; what had happened made a man of him overnight. Since then his guns had backed the law, and had earned him a deep-seated respect from the Río Grande to the Platte, from the Rockies to the Missouri.

Wardow's letter telling of Hogan's death had brought him here; he had ridden in with a vague foreboding of what was to come. This was it, then—he was face to face with the greatest problem of his life. He eased back onto the desk and sat there, considering what Wardow had said. He would kill this man. But how?

Beneath him he felt the prod of the spur rowel; he reached down and took it in his hand. *It'll build a rope necktie for some poor jasper,* he mused. *Jim, you snake belly, you brought me into something here.* Then, idly, his mind toyed with the idea of going through with the thing. That thought inspired another, until finally a wry smile wreathed his features.

A hint of that same smile still lingered five minutes later when Tade Wardow opened his eyes and stared up at him blankly. The banker's first instinctive gesture was to raise a hand to ease the pain in his head. When he recognized Lonesome, a sneer twisted his features into ugliness.

"I looked for this," he snarled. "A week ago I gave Sheriff Mays an envelope. Jim Hogan's confession is sealed up in it. If anything happens to me, Mays opens it."

"So there's a reward still out for the Tentpole killing?" Lonesome asked levelly.

"Three thousand, and what Mays has will put every lawman in Arizona on the prod for you." He came stiffly to his feet as he spoke, glaring defiantly. "Take it or leave it, Barkley. Do this my way, and you clear out of here with eleven thousand. Do it yours . . . and you'll hang."

Strangely enough, Lonesome smiled and shrugged. "I'm listening, Wardow. Only I didn't like what you said a while back. You know too much."

"I've said you're safe with me. Play along on this and you'll come off a free man."

Lonesome didn't answer. Wardow waited a brief moment, then asked: "Are you in with me?"

"What about the envelope you gave your lawman?"

The banker smiled smugly: "He keeps that. Something could happen to me later on." He was no longer afraid, believing himself safe so long as he possessed this evidence against Lonesome.

"That's a tough bargain, Wardow."

"Take it or leave it," the banker repeated.

Lonesome looked down at the spur rowel resting in his palm and seemed to consider what Wardow had said. At length, he drawled: "What do I do?"

"Come to my place, the white house out at the east end of the street, at nine tonight. I'll give you enough dynamite to touch off so that it'll look like a real job. You'll find the money in sacks on the floor at the back of the vault. Leave the money sacks and the rowel on the floor, inside. Close the vault door, don't lock it, set the dynamite, and ride away from here. And you never saw me, Lonesome."

"But why do I leave this?" Lonesome indicated the pointed

bit of steel in his palm.

"There's a thing or two in this world money won't buy. That's going to get me one of 'em."

If Wardow had known his man, he would have been suspicious when Lonesome reached back to take the card from the desk and put it and the spur rowel in his pocket, saying meekly: "I'll be there at nine."

The banker's arrogant smile returned as the door swung shut behind Lonesome, and the light of a full confidence crept back into his eyes. He was once more his old self.

II

From where he stood under the sidewalk awning, Lonesome looked across the street and up to the second-story window, lettered DR. SILAS HOYER. Yet it was a good five minutes before he finally went across and climbed the stairs to the doctor's office. Inside, he found a portly, gray-haired man drowsing in a swivel chair. His worn boots were propped on an untidy desk.

Doc Hoyer opened his eyes at the sound of the closing door, glanced at his visitor, and muttered gruffly: "You don't look sick."

"I reckon I don't. But I've got a cough, Doc. Tell me what to do for it."

The sawbones swiveled around and dropped his feet to the floor. "A pint of Red-Eye Barton's bourbon is the best thing for a cough. Let's hear it once."

Lonesome coughed, gently. Even so, Hoyer's eyes narrowed in studied inscrutability. He shrugged and stood up, saying casually: "Peel off your shirt and I'll have a look."

He went over Lonesome's chest, laying his palm flat against it and tapping the fingers of that hand with the stiff third finger of his other. Finally he stepped back and looked at his patient:

"Like I told you, a pint of liquor's what you need. Hell, you big strapping cusses come in here if you cut your finger. It'll cost you two dollars this time, stranger." His tone was gruff but now there was a softness behind the look in his honest brown eyes that he couldn't hide. Lonesome caught it, and in it had his answer.

"How much longer will you give me, Doc? A year?" he asked quietly.

Hoyer's expression hardened. "You're talking like a damned fool. Your lungs are sound, man. A good rest might not hurt. Plenty of eggs and milk and good food, and you'll be here to bounce your grandchildren on your knee."

Lonesome only half heard what Hoyer was saying. He was staring vacantly out the window and down onto the street. It was what he expected. His answer lay in Hoyer's look, and now he felt strangely relieved for the certainty it gave him. Perhaps it was because he'd known it for so long that he could feel no regret. His life had been like his name—he was a lonesome man. Beyond a very few real friends, he had no one to make it hard to face what was coming—no woman he loved, no family. There was one man, had he lived, a young cowboy from Wyoming who had ridden with Lonesome into the death that was pounding madly in a thundering stampede. The youngster never came out again; Lonesome did, and owed him for his life that wild night of storm. How many years ago had that been?

His glance shuttled on up the street to the brick front of the bank, and his thoughts for the moment centered on the bank, on Tade Wardow, and on the part each was to play in what was planned. Thinking of the man, it surprised him to see Wardow step out of the bank entrance at that very moment and turn to come down the opposite walk toward him.

Lonesome watched the banker, feeling again a deep-rooted hatred toward him. He watched until Wardow, almost directly across the street now, stopped, and tipped his low-crowned hat to a girl coming down the walk. It was the girl who took Lonesome's eye then. She wore a brown skirt, a bright yellow blouse, and was hatless. Frankly studying her, Lonesome was instantly aware of the subtle beauty of her slim figure and tawny hair and light, creamy skin.

"Who is she?" he asked aloud. "Looks sort of like I'd seen her before." And yet he knew he couldn't have.

"Who?" Hoyer asked, coming to stand alongside Lonesome. "Oh, Mary Latrobe? She's a good friend of mine. And she's talking to the biggest skunk that ever walked on his hind legs."

Lonesome waited for more, surprised and interested at the doctor's blunt outburst. But Hoyer stood there in a frowning silence, glaring at Tade Wardow and the girl.

"Sounds like you don't take to him," Lonesome offered.

"No. I know him better than most. He owns half the town and the county and is trying awful hard to get the other half. Like I said before, Tade Wardow's a prime polecat. Not that it would interest you."

"What about the girl, Mary Latrobe? Is she his, too?"

"Not by a damned sight. He'd like to have her, but Ed Hardy has something to say about that."

"Who's Ed Hardy?"

Hoyer looked up at him, his glance faintly quizzical. "There's no reason why I should be running off at the mouth to a stranger. Who's Ed Hardy? He's a poor, busted, hard-working devil who's in love with that girl over there. She's in love with him, too, but they can't get spliced. Ed's got a mortgage on his outfit . . . couple of thousand dollars . . . and stands a good chance of spending the rest of his life working it off. They say he'll lose his shirt this fall. I wouldn't know for sure."

"Now don't tell me that this ranny across here . . . Wardow . . . holds the mortgage."

"How did you know?" Hoyer asked, chuckling grimly. "Wardow's the banker here. Yes, he holds the mortgage. And he'd be the first one to close out on Ed."

The two of them stood there in silence, watching Tade Wardow as he once more tipped his hat to Mary Latrobe and stepped to one side to let her walk on past him and up the street. So Mary Latrobe was what Wardow's money couldn't buy. It was almost as if fate had blazed his path into this town. Again the memory of that night, years ago, came to him when a young cowpuncher named Red Latrobe had gone down under the thousand knife-sharp hoofs of that mad herd. Gone to die so that Lonesome Barkley might live.

Piece by piece Lonesome was fitting together the puzzle that had come out of his visit to the bank. He was thinking of the spur rowel, too, thinking that a spur is a thing that pretty accurately labels a man. There were exceptions, of course, but ordinarily a man with money would wear something better on a pair of fine boots than the plain piece of steel Wardow had given him. This rowel fit a spur a man could buy for $1.50 a pair at any hardware store. It was plain and worn and hardly one to be one used by a particular man.

Dipping a hand into his pocket for the money he owed the doctor, he felt the cold chill of the steel. And suddenly he knew what Tade Wardow was trying to do. It was Ed Hardy who was being framed—framed because he loved the girl Tade Wardow wanted.

"Here's your money, Doc. Maybe this Ed Hardy won't lose out after all."

"You're wrong about that," was Hoyer's grim answer. "Anyone who bucks Wardow loses out. It'll take time, but Mary Latrobe will be Missus Wardow one of these days, and Ed'll be moving away to try the grass on some other range. It's a hell of a world."

"Would you trade places with me?"

Hoyer's grizzled countenance flushed a trifle. He smiled thinly. "You aren't so bad off, stranger. You aren't so bad off."

At 3:00 that afternoon, a loquacious oldster down at the livery stable pointed out Ed Hardy to the stranger without knowing he'd done it. At 5:00 Lonesome saw Hardy go in through the swing doors of Red-Eye Barton's saloon. By 6:30 he had finished a leisurely supper and was standing at the bar in Red-Eye's place.

Lonesome stood there twenty minutes, took three drinks of bourbon straight, and then sauntered back to look in on the poker game at the back table. Ed Hardy was in the game, so was Doc Hoyer. Ten minutes later Hoyer turned and looked up to see who was standing behind his chair. He smiled pleasantly as he recognized his patient.

"Want to sit in, stranger? It's penny ante. We don't lose much and we don't win much."

"Suits me," Lonesome answered. "I'll stay till I use up this dollar."

He went around the table and took a chair backed by the wall. At any other time the force of the long habit would have prompted him to do this, but now he did it because it put him directly across the table from Ed Hardy. The fog of tobacco smoke that hung over the table bit into Lonesome's lungs and made him cough several times. Once he caught Hoyer's pointed scrutiny. The doctor's eyes abruptly shifted when they met his, and Lonesome smiled, knowing what the other was thinking.

Doc Hoyer was the oldest man at the table. The three others were men of Hardy's age, young and clean-looking and obviously playing for the enjoyment of the low-stake game. In all Lonesome's experience he had never found a thing that so quickly and accurately mirrors a man's character as a game of poker. For that reason he watched how Ed Hardy played his cards. When it was his own turn to deal, he invariably called for a hand of stud. A man showed more at stud than he did at draw.

In less than half an hour he learned that Hardy's game was a conservative one, balanced with an occasional bluff hand that would have made him dangerous at high stakes. On one hand of draw, Hardy stole a pot against Doc Hoyer, betting the limit each raise until the sawbones threw down his three kings, face up, growling: "You've got 'em or you wouldn't bet. If you'd only play Mary that way, Ed. You don't have a damned thing to lose."

Hardy smiled, a smile that would have been mirthless but for his open friendliness toward Hoyer. He reached out and raked in the stack of chips, saying: "Nothing to lose? No, I reckon I haven't, Doc. But she has. A two-bit cow nurse like me doesn't have much to offer."

Hoyer snorted. "In my day a man didn't let things like that bother him. It's your deal, stranger."

Lonesome had the feeling that Hoyer had mentioned this to remind him of their conversation that morning. Regardless of Hoyer's motives, he had prompted an answer from Ed Hardy that was pregnant in its meaning—an answer that somehow settled things in Lonesome's mind. He watched Hardy closely after that, seeing the hint of a worried frown that wrinkled the man's high forehead under his sandy hair. Mention of Mary Latrobe had put that frown there, and, when it didn't disappear with Hardy's winning several hands, Lonesome knew that the worry was so deep-rooted within the man that it would eventually become a part of his make-up.

At 8:30 his mind was decided. He tilted back in his chair, drawling: "Cash me in, gents. I may be back later on." He had lost 67¢ and had enjoyed the game as much as any he could remember.

Outside, Lonesome walked on up the street to a point beyond the lit store windows before he cut across and into an alley and started back toward the center of town. It lacked half an hour of the time Tade Wardow had set for their meeting. He didn't know what lay ahead, and for that reason he hurried now, walking silently in the deep shadows as the looming bulk of the back brick wall of the bank rose out of the darkness ahead.

The door should be open, he mused. *He wants to make it easy for me.*

His guess was borne out a moment later as he tried the knob on the door. It swung in soundlessly on well-oiled hinges and he stepped quickly in and closed it behind him, one of his six-shooters in a hand planted at his hip. He stepped noiselessly to one side of the door and stood there a full minute, listening and identifying the sounds that came to him. Somewhere up front a clock ticked slowly. He waited until his hearing became accustomed to the sound, until he could hear beyond it. Then there was nothing but dead silence.

He moved on in, stepping around the end of the counter. He could pick out the cobalt rectangle of the vault door against the lighter shade of the tan wall. His glance shuttled over each subject in the cleared space behind the cages, identifying it, searching the shadows. Finally he was satisfied, and dropped his weapon back into its holster.

Putting his head close to the dial on the vault door, he vaguely made out the numbers on it. That afternoon he had memorized the combination Wardow had given him, and then had burned the card. Now he spun the dial carefully, knowing that a mistake would cost him precious seconds. When he caught the faint sound of the tumbler click that told him the lock was open, he felt a wave of relief surge through him. Wardow might be framing a man, but he was playing straight with Lonesome Barkley.

He put his weight against the thick handle of the vault door and felt it give under the pressure. The massive steel panel was heavy and it took a good bit of his strength to swing it open. The exertion brought on that feeling of constriction in his lungs, and he coughed twice, softly, muffling the sound with his bandanna held at his mouth.

With the door closed behind him, he lit a match. In the sudden flood of light he saw the money sacks piled on the floor against the rear wall of the vault.

Eleven thousand dollars. A man could buy a nice layout for that. He could take things easy for a few years, Lonesome thought.

The temptation was undeniably there, but he stifled it down as he set to work in the darkness. He emptied the sacks, piling the bundles of crisp banknotes onto the floor behind him. Once he went out of the vault and spent two full minutes hunting until he found an empty ledger box. He brought it back inside and piled the money into it. Then, carrying the box, he came out again and shut the vault door.

He made his exit soundlessly, but this time he walked down the alley in the direction opposite the way he had come, carrying the box. Five minutes later he came within sight of a large white frame house at the end of the street, looking gray under the starlight. Here, behind the house and close to him, lay the sprawled outline of a shed.

It was what he wanted. He went inside, with a gun in one hand and the box under his other arm. After setting the box down, he risked lighting a match, flicking it out when he'd glimpsed the shiny new buggy standing to one side, ahead of two vacant stalls. He crossed over to the buggy and lifted the seat cushion. Beneath it, his groping hand ran around an empty locker. Five seconds later he had hefted the box into the compartment and put the seat cushion back into place, so that the box was hidden beneath it. This would have to do. It was an even better hiding place than he had hoped.

Outside once more, he made a wide circle of the house, keeping out of sight in the darkness until he came to the street. When he approached the house again, he came along the front walk, moving at a slow easy pace, and made no attempt to hide his coming.

Wardow answered his knock, opening the door stealthily on an unlit room so that his well-fed, plump figure showed only for an instant before he stepped back into the shadows. Lonesome went in, heard the door close softly behind him, and felt Wardow's hand on his arm as he was led toward the back of the house.

They went through an inner door. Wardow's hold relaxed and he said: "Wait. I'll get a light."

In another moment a match flared in his hand. He touched the flame to the wick of a lamp, and immediately Lonesome saw that he was in a high-ceilinged kitchen. The shades were drawn tightly down over the two windows. The precautions Wardow was taking brought a twisted smile to Lonesome's thin lips.

"You're spooky, tonight, Wardow."

"Careful is all," the banker answered. His full, round face had a measure of that same paleness Lonesome had seen that morning. When he moved now, he did so with the jerky motions of a pent-up nervousness. He pointed to a bundle of three wrapped sticks of dynamite and a four-foot length of fuse lying on the table in the center of the room. "Set that off at the base of the vault door. The fuse is long enough to give you a five-minute start. The back door of the bank's open. You won't have any trouble."

Lonesome nodded, his glance holding a faint hint of intolerance. "Is there anything else?"

"Remember what you're leaving on the floor with those money sacks."

Again Lonesome nodded.

Apparently his studied calmness bolstered Wardow's courage. For a fleeting moment all trace of fear went out of the banker's eyes. "I won't forget this, Lonesome," he said.

"Neither will I. Eleven thousand is a lot of money. I come out the best on this deal."

The smile that crossed Wardow's countenance meant more than he intended. He faced the table and handed Lonesome the dynamite, reaching back again to turn down the lamp. Then he crossed to the door, inched it open, and said: "Take the alley. It leads to the bank."

"In twenty minutes I'll be a mile out on the trail into the hills," Lonesome told him as he went out. "You can time it if you want."

It took him only three minutes to reach the bank again. He moved surely this time, putting the dynamite at the base of the vault door as Wardow had directed. It took him little more than a minute to be sure everything was just so. Then he lit the fuse.

As the powder flame hissed across the dead silence, he stood there, watching it. He waited until it had burned for better than a foot of its length, leaving a charred black ash. Then, carefully, he smothered the flame beneath his boot sole and waited for a full half minute longer, making sure that it had died.

III

Sheriff John Mays looked up as the door to his office opened. The stranger he had seen riding in on the dun stallion that morning stood there. He took his pipe out of his mouth and said: " 'Evening, stranger."

Lonesome nodded an answer to the greeting, then asked

27

abruptly: "Should anyone be in the bank at this time of night, Sheriff?"

Mays frowned, puzzled. "No. Why?"

"I went over there to look in at the clock a few minutes ago, and saw a man moving around back by the vault. I thought you ought to know about it."

The lawman's spare figure lunged up out of his swivel chair. He reached for his gun belt, swung it off his desk and around his waist. "Why didn't you holler? He's probably gone now, with the mine payroll."

"I did better than that," Lonesome told him. "I waited in the alley out back until he came out. I followed him to a big white house at the edge of town. He carried a box away with him."

Mays sat down abruptly, sighing his relief. All the tension had suddenly left him. He laughed softly. "Goddlemighty, but you had me scared, stranger. The man you saw was Tade War-dow, president of the bank. He lives in that big house at the end of the street. He was probably working late at his office."

"But what was he carrying?" Lonesome asked, his expression bewildered.

"Books . . . ledgers, probably. He carts 'em home 'most every night."

Lonesome grinned guiltily, shrugged, and turned to the door. "My mistake," he said. Then a frown crossed his face, as though he had thought of something. "You'd better tell this Wardow to be more careful, Sheriff. He left the back door of the bank open. I know, because I tried it on my way back here."

"That's not like Tade," Mays muttered, rising again. "I'd better go take a look. Want to come along?"

Lonesome shook his head: "It probably won't amount to much. I'm due back in a game of draw across the street."

He walked with the lawman to a point opposite Barton's and left him, crossing the street and waiting there until the other had disappeared into the opening between the bank and the adjoining building. Once the sheriff was out of sight, he went on unhurriedly up the street. Beyond the stores, his pace quickened. He re-crossed the street to a vacant lot, cut through it, and back to the alley once more. He'd hide in the shed in back of Tade Wardow's and wait there for the sheriff.

With the shed in sight once more—a black, squat shape showing against the lighter shade of the yard surrounding it—Lonesome stopped for a few brief seconds to listen. The night sounds were strangely magnified. Somewhere in the distance a dog howled mournfully; he plainly heard the hoof pound of a trotting horse far down the street, and even the sound of his own breathing was loud in his ears.

He was tuned to a high-pitched wariness as he walked on toward the shed. The hinged double door was as he had left it, standing open a good three feet so that he could walk through without having to move it. Inside, the darkness was impenetrable. Trying to remember what he had seen in the brief glow of the match on his first visit, he was about to move out of the door when an indefinable sound shuttled across the stillness ahead.

"Hold it, Lonesome!"

It was Tade Wardow's low voice!

Lonesome froze where he stood, instinctively realizing that he was outlined by the faint light of the open door behind. The hackles rose along the back of his neck. It wasn't fear he felt, but a tense expectancy of the blast of Tade Wardow's gun, for the man must have a gun lined at him.

"Shuck out your hardware," came Wardow's ominous words. "And take it slow!"

There was no choice. Lonesome lifted his two .38s out of the holsters and dropped them so that they thudded hollowly against the rough planking of the floor. He timed his motions to an awkward slowness, remembering the make-up of the man who stood there ahead of him in the darkness.

"So you'd double-cross me, would you?" Wardow asked softly. "It was a good hunch . . . coming out here to watch after you'd gone." He paused there, until the silence suspended unbearably. Then: "How did you frame me?"

"Mays is on his way here."

He spoke with a grim purpose backing the words. He was trying to rouse Wardow's anger.

"That means I'll have to get rid of you both," said Wardow, his words edged with a faintly recognizable panic. "It'll look like the two of you shot it out."

"It won't work. Mays will come to the house . . . the front."

"It will work. When I cut loose on you, he'll come back here."

Lonesome was staring in the direction of the voice, his perceptions keyed to an alertness that caught every hint of sound. The slight scraping of one of Wardow's boots on the floor helped along with the voice. He knew where the man stood now; the buggy's front wheel-hub would be directly behind him.

"And the bank? What about that?"

"I'll find the money and take it back. You must have brought. . . ."

Before the words were completed, Lonesome lunged in a rolling dive. A blasting explosion ripped across the silence, and Lonesome felt the air rush of the bullet as it whipped past his face. And then he was slamming into Wardow's yielding body.

As they crashed together to the floor, the purple-flamed thunder of the gun cut loose again. And with that inferno of sound Lonesome felt the tensed muscles of Wardow's body beneath him jerk once in a writhing spasm. Wardow choked out a stifled groan and went suddenly limp. And when Lonesome pushed himself to his knees and reached for a match and lit it, he saw the answer.

The banker's right elbow had slammed against the wheel hub of the buggy as he fell, twisting the six-gun into his side. The blow had knocked his thumb from the hammer of the weapon. A wisp of smoke curled up from the torn, blood-soaked cloth of Wardow's coat. He was dead.

It was while he kneeled there that he heard the pounding of boots in the gravel outside. Up front, behind one of the stalls, he had seen a narrow door. He came to his feet, stooped to pick up his guns, smothered the match, and made for that door. He was none too soon, for as he stepped through the door and eased it shut again he heard Mays's strident challenge from the alley out back.

Lonesome tried to move soundlessly, as he crossed the strip of yard in back of the house and turned the corner to put himself out of sight of the shed. All the while a growing, insistent constriction in his overworked lungs made him want to cough. He choked it back until he had crossed the road out front. There, he gave in to it, once more muffling his deep hacking with the bandanna pressed to his lips.

He waited there a long quarter minute before he moved on. No sounds came from behind the house. Mays was being quiet about his discovery. He wasn't to learn the reason until later.

Going back to Barton's saloon, Lonesome skirted the rear of the houses that flanked the street. He passed the stores, and went beyond them before he returned to the boardwalk. When he entered the saloon, he had come from the direction opposite to that of Tade Wardow's house.

"Back to make a cleaning?" Doc Hoyer grinned as Lonesome sauntered up to the table and took the chair he had vacated earlier.

Lonesome nodded, throwing a silver dollar onto the green felt table top. Hoyer was banker, and counted him out his chips, asking: "Did you hear a couple shots out there a while back?"

"Must have been someone out beyond town taking a lick at a coyote," Lonesome answered.

He won the first hand, and he won the second. His expression was sober as he looked at his cards, belying the tumult of expectancy within him. He was waiting for Ed Hardy's turn at the deal, thinking of the $3,000 reward still out for the stage robbery at Tentpole, thinking that the money would mean a lot to a man trying to make a go of a small outfit.

It was Ed Hardy's deal. A perfect calm settled through Lonesome Barkley as he watched Hardy gather in the cards and shuffle the deck. It was as though he had never left the game, as though the happenings of the last forty minutes had not been shaped for these next few seconds. Suddenly he heard Doc Hoyer say: "Here comes John Mays. He looks like trouble."

Mays was already halfway between the door up front and the table. They looked at him with a rising curiosity at the worried expression of the lawman's grizzled face. Lonesome's expression showed bitter disappointment overriding every other emotion. He had planned this, planned it carefully, but Mays had come in a little too soon.

Mays stopped, standing behind Ed Hardy. Seeing that the shcriff's glance had settled on him, Lonesome lost all hope. Mays knew. He had been to his office and read Jim Hogan's confession.

Then Mays was speaking to him: "You were right, stranger. The bank was held up. But I was right, too. Tade Wardow was the man you saw. I went out to see him and he heard me coming and shot himself. Blew a hole through his side. I found the money hidden in his buggy out in the shed behind the house."

Mays went on, speaking to the others now, leaning down over the table and talking quietly so that those at the bar up front wouldn't hear. He didn't want the news to get out, he said, until he'd had time to see the bank directors in the morning. People were liable to be spooky and think something was wrong about the bank. It might stir up trouble if they found out tonight. He told about discovering the dynamite and the fuse that Tade Wardow had lit. Still unable to believe that it had been Wardow, he'd gone out to his house to see him and heard the shots as he was coming along the alley.

"But why would Tade do a thing like that?" Doc Hoyer asked as the lawman finished.

Mays shrugged and threw out his hands in an unknown gesture. "That's what I can't figure. Insurance, maybe. He came to me a couple of weeks ago and gave me a sealed envelope. Told me to open it if anything happened to him, that he was expecting trouble. This must be what he meant. I'm going over now to open it and see what's inside. You go ahead with the game and don't let on anything's happened. Above all, I don't want this to get out."

He turned and walked across the room and out the door. Lonesome, his hopes alive once more, said briefly: "It's your deal, Hardy."

They were all silent as Ed Hardy shuffled the cards and passed the deck to Doc Hoyer for the cut. The news that Mays had brought had left them stunned. Ed Hardy moved his hands automatically, and Hoyer cursed softly time and again as though unable to comprehend what he'd heard. Hardy dealt a hand of draw. Doc Hoyer opened, and Lonesome and Ed Hardy and one of the others covered his bet. Hardy filled in the other hands, raked in the discards, and then dealt himself two cards. As he laid the deck on the table, Lonesome lunged up out of his chair, kicked it from behind him so that it crashed into the wall, and drawled: "Hold it, Hardy! You palmed that last card!"

Five pairs of eyes swiveled up to stare at Lonesome in hard disbelief. He stood there glaring across at Hardy, whose face took in a quick flush at the insult.

"You're loco, stranger," he said. "I wouldn't know how to palm a card."

"Will you get onto your feet, or do I have to blow out your guts where you sit."

Every muscle in Ed Hardy's body became taut. The words hit him like a blow in the face. He started up out of his chair, and shook off the hand Doc Hoyer put out to stop him. Lonesome Barkley cleared his throat and coughed, gently, as though the words he had just spoken had torn something loose inside him. He hunched over a little, his flat chest rising and falling noticeably as he caught his breath.

Then they were moving, Hardy clawing at his holstered .45 in a frantic haste, and Lonesome's hand streaking to his own weapon in a blur of practiced speed. His six-shooter had cleared leather when another coughing spasm hit him. A deep-chested hacking doubled him up, broke the smooth flow of his gun arm. Ed Hardy's .45 nosed up and darted flame in a blasting roar. Lonesome's Colt thundered an answer but, stooped over as he was, his aim was wide. They saw the bullet hit, jerking Lonesome backward so that he fell into the wall and slid slowly to the floor as his knees buckled. The expression on his face held no trace of surprise as Doc Hoyer came around the table and looked down at him. The others stepped in beside Ed Hardy and took his gun away from him.

Hoyer had one look at the blood that flecked Lonesome's lips, at the red smear that crept out across his shirt front, and gazed up at the others, shaking his head slowly. Then he leaned down and asked: "Why did you do it, stranger? Ed Hardy never cheated at anything."

"Maybe I didn't see right," came Lonesome's whispered answer. "I wanted to win that hand."

"A fifty-cent hand?"

"Lay off, Doc. Come closer." When Doc's ear was close to his mouth, Lonesome said: "There's three thousand on my head. Is that enough?"

Silas Hoyer's tough old face softened. He glanced obliquely at Ed Hardy and then back at Lonesome. "It's plenty," he said huskily. "Plenty."

Lonesome closed his eyes and smiled. It would be enough, too, to square a debt to the kid sister of a young cowboy called Red Latrobe who had died one night, years ago, in the Bar X stampede. And even after the rise and fall of his flat chest had ceased, the smile still held. . . .

★ ★ ★ ★ ★

RETIREMENT DAY

★ ★ ★ ★ ★

The author titled this story "Retirement Day". It was submitted by his agent to Popular Publications on February 11, 1939, where it remained for more than two years in what was termed at magazines as the slush pile, made up of stories that might be used someday. In this case the Peter Dawson story was first purchased on November 29, 1941 to appear in the second issue of a new Western pulp magazine titled *Western Tales* (2/42). This was also the last issue before the name of the magazine was changed to *Fifteen Western Tales,* in which guise it would continue for 115 issues until 1955. The author was paid $45 at the rate of 1¢ a word. "Retirement Day" is also available in a full-cast dramatization with music and sound effects in *Great American Westerns: Volume Four* from Graphic Audio.

Slim, the apron, poured out a double shot of rye whiskey and told old Joe Miles: "This is on the house, Joe. For old time's sake."

The half dozen men at the bar heard Slim and tried not to look at Joe, making small talk among themselves and not doing it very well.

When old Joe said—"So long, boys. See you . . . well, see you one of these days."—they bid him good bye with a forced cheerfulness and were relieved when the swing doors up front hid his stooped slat of a figure.

"To hell with the railroad!" Slim grunted, rinsing Joe's glass and toweling it viciously. "To hell with all these new-fangled ideas! There's probably the last time we'll ever lay eyes on that old jasper. He's still a good man and they're kickin' him out."

"He's sixty-seven," someone ventured.

"He's as old as he thinks he is." Slim glowered at the speaker. "And until they gave him the sack, he was younger'n me or you. Listen here, brother"—Slim leaned across the bar and wagged a forefinger in the man's face, not caring that his customer was a comparative newcomer and didn't know Joe Miles as well as the rest did—"I've seen that old fool work three nights runnin' without sleep, freightin' food in here from the railhead through a blizzard you'd be scared to stick your nose out into. I've seen him take a three-team stage over a washed-out hill trail you'd balk at walkin' a mule across. Don't tell me Joe's no good any more. When his old heart stops pumping, when they've throwed six feet of dirt on him, then he'll be ready to retire."

A stillness settled over the nearly empty saloon. No one else had a word to say. It was, in a way, the most fitting tribute paid Joe Miles that day.

Going along the street toward the stage station, old Joe hunched up his narrow shoulders and tilted his head down, so that the rain didn't hit his face but instead trickled down off the limp brim of his wide Stetson. He felt tired today, utterly weary for the first time in his keen memory. Maybe he was getting too old, like they said. He let himself get only so far along that line of thinking before he grumbled a ripe oath and hurried on.

He turned in off the walk at the office of the Blue Star Stage Lines, a weathered frame shack at the front of a huge hump-roofed barn. The man behind the wicket looked up from under his green eye shade as Joe came in and said in an embarrassed attempt at joking: "It'd spoil things if you had good weather for your last run, eh?"

The oldster snorted, shook the rain from his coat. "What're they doing with you, Len?"

"Making me bookkeeper down at Sands. I go down Tuesday, by train."

"Reckon I ought to ride the blamed thing myself just to see what it's like," old Joe said, smiling wryly, his lips a thin line below his corn-silk longhorn mustache. "Maybe I ought to ask the railroad for a job, seeing as how they done me right plumb out of this one."

The door opened and a tall, rangy man strode in, shaking the rain off his slicker. This was Ray Dineen, thirty and married. For ten years he had ridden shotgun alongside old Joe on the stage run out of this mining camp to Sands, the town on the plain, where the Blue Star had its division office, halfway along its main line.

Ray was making this last trip down with old Joe today, riding shotgun on the bank's regular week-end payroll shipment. Rumor had it that the money chest would contain an additional $14,000 in gold for the railroad crew working out of Sands. There wasn't going to be any fuss taking it through, since the rail officials weren't anxious to attract attention. Starting next week, the new spur would be finished and they would be sending trains through here and down to Sands and this short branch of the Blue Star Lines would be a thing of the past.

Ray Dineen said—"Hi, ya, Joe."—and his face was serious. He had something to say and didn't know how to say it. Finally he blurted out: "I did every damn' thing I could, Joe. Saw that young pup, Ted Baker, the new superintendent. What a boss! My age, and he's ordering around men old enough to be his father." He shook his head soberly. "It's no use, Joe. Baker claims you're too old. He brought up that business about our getting drunk down in Vegas last December, too. Said I was lucky to be staying on after what happened."

Old Joe nodded. "Maybe we did raise too much sand that night. But we got here on time, didn't we, drunk or sober? And we didn't kill no horses or wreck no equipment." He shrugged, as though dismissing the thought. "What have they lined up for you, Ray?"

A little of his inward pride couldn't help but show in Ray Dineen's eyes. "They're giving me a try at the ribbons."

Old Joe's eyes lighted up. He smacked a fist into an open palm. "Driving? The main line. Ray, there's big pay, a future. I'll give you ten years before they make you division superintendent."

Ray shook his head. "That's the job they should be giving you. Hell, you deserve it. I don't."

"Don't go soft-hearted for me," Joe said. "I got plans for the future. Besides, I got a notion I ought to retire, live on my savings."

"What savings? You borrowed twenty from me last pay day." Ray Dineen's square face took on a bulldog look. But then he saw the pointlessness of the argument, swore, and said: "Let's get her rolling. They're waiting out there on the walk by the bank. They'll be sore if we don't hurry."

Five minutes later, slicker on, his Stetson pulled down hard on his ears, old Joe wheeled the Concord down off the barn ramp and led his two half-wild teams of Morgans downstreet under tight rein. No passengers were along this trip. Lately the load had been mostly freight, as today. Ray Dineen sat beside Joe, a double-barreled Greener cradled across his knees. As the Concord pulled in at the edge of the walk by the bank, where four guards waited with a brass-bound money chest, the rain was coming down in a relentless spray whipped by the wind. The street was a sea of mud, fetlock deep to the horses; the town had a bedraggled, sodden look about it.

"Sling her up here where we can keep an eye on her!" Joe shouted to the guards, pitching his voice to carry above the drone of rain on a nearby tin roof. He and Ray reached down, got a hold on one of the chest's leather handles, and heaved it up into the boot beneath them.

While Ray lashed it in place with a length of half-inch rope, Joe called—"Of course we'll make it!"—in answer to a question Len Rivers, president of the bank, shouted from the doorway.

The teams slogged into the pull a moment later, and the Concord rolled out from the walk and down the street, past the stores and the awninged walks, past the few brick and frame houses and the many tar-paper shacks along the cañon slopes, and finally out past the shaft houses of the Dolly Madison and Wee Willie mines.

Then the town lay behind and the stage was rolling along a

winding trail through the high pines and scrubby cedars. Old Joe hadn't paid the town much attention purposely, for he hated good byes and knew he might never again see the place he'd called home for thirty-four years. He'd live down in Sands from now on, get a cheap room, and be handy for a job if any came along. The railroad was hiring men at pick and shovel work along the new right of way. Maybe they'd take him on.

"What did Rivers say?" Ray Dineen shouted above the downpour and the rattle of doubletree chains and the creaking of harness.

"Asked me if I thought we could get across Graveyard Wash," old Joe growled. "As though I hadn't been driving this road long enough to know!"

Ray frowned. "I wondered about that myself. Sue and the kids are ahead somewhere in the wagon. They want to get to Sands before dark."

"They'll make it," old Joe said, expertly concealing the instant tightening of worry inside him. Sue Dineen and Ray's kids, Ellen and young Tommy, heading down out of the mountains in a storm like this? Sue with a wagonload of goods, furniture, bedding, all their worldly possessions. And she a frail woman at that, barely able to manage a team.

He was blaming Ray when he remembered that at 1:00, two hours ago, the sun had been shining on a balmy summer afternoon. This had been one of those freak summer storms, with the clouds piling up behind the peaks for the last two days and spilling their rain when they rolled on over the mountains to hit the cold updrafts on this side. It would be a good long rain if old Joe's weather eye was cocked right.

Joe decided not to worry. Sue had good enough sense not to head across Graveyard Wash if there was any water running. It was different with an old hand like him. He'd cheated the Graveyard more times than he could count on his gnarled fingers and crooked toes. He'd learned to gauge the water that foamed along the bed of that hundred-yard-wide wash that ran a torrent each time it even sprinkled in the hills. He'd taken his stage across many a time with half a day's traffic of riders and wagons and rigs held up on the road on each side, all afraid to tackle the surging flood of water. Once he'd caught hell for it from the superintendent when the water boiled in over the floor below and soiled the dress of a woman passenger.

Four miles downcañon old Joe hit the first washout in the trail, with a fifty-foot drop to the cañon bottom on one side and a sheer climbing wall on the other. The Concord swayed dangerously, but was righted with perfect precision as Joe flicked one on-wheeler's rump with his whip and made the animal lunge into the pull. As the right rear wheel hit solid ground again and jarred the vehicle clear to the thorough braces, Ray Dineen suddenly groaned and doubled up with pain. He straightened a second later, but not before old Joe had turned a glance to see his rugged face white and lined in agony.

Old Joe tightened the ribbons and drove home the brake. "Bouncing too much, Ray?" he called.

Ray shook his head. "Gut ache. It must be something. . . ." A gripping pain took him and he broke off his words and doubled over once more. His hand went to his side, below his belt. Then he caught himself and straightened up, taking his hand away. "Go on. I'll be all right in a minute or two."

"We'll stop at Ford's," Joe said. He knew the signs, had seen men taken with appendicitis before. He was wondering how long it would take John Ford to hitch his team to his buckboard and get Ray back to town. One thing they could all be thankful for was young Doc Slade, the physician who'd come in last year and started healing people instead of feeding them those sugar pills old Doc Wheelwright had left in his office when he died.

They drove in at Ford's, a thirty-acre ranch in a clearing

along the cañon, a quarter hour later. By that time the pain had hit Ray once again, and then eased off.

Ray was stubborn and wanted to go on.

"What'll Sue and the kids do without me?" he kept insisting.

"I'll look after Sue," old Joe said. He met John Ford halfway between the yard fence and the house, explaining what he wanted.

"Sure, I'll take him in, right away," Ford agreed. Joe turned and started back toward the Concord, but Ford reached out and took a hold on his arm, saying in a lower voice: "But there's something you ought to know before you go on, Joe. Chet Richter and Barney Ryan went past here about an hour ago, headed out to the road."

"What have them two tramps got to do with this? I tell you Ray's sick, John. You hurry and get that team harnessed." He started out across the yard again.

"Listen, you bull-headed old fool!" Ford called. "Think a minute. I said Chet Richter and Barney Ryan. You're carrying the railroad's gold, ain't you?"

"And I'll be carrying you out to that wagon shed unless you get a sudden move on."

"Chet and Barney were fired last Tuesday for trying to lead the crew out on strike. They've been trying to work off their grudge against Paul Duval all week. Don't that mean nothing to you?"

It did. Old Joe finally got it. What Ford could have said in as few words was that Chet Richter and Barney Ryan were a couple of hardcases, that they'd been fired for making trouble for Paul Duval, boss of the section gang working the railroad right of way below town, and that it wasn't out of the realm of possibility to suppose that they'd try and hold up the stage on the road and get even with Duval and the owners.

Old Joe faced John Ford with an angry light blazing in his

watery blue eyes. He was worried, tired, and his patience was worn thin. "John, you ain't never got over shooting that rustler twenty years ago. These ain't the old days. If Chet and Barney laid so much as a finger on that money chest, they'd have every railroad detective this side of Kansas City out after 'em. Now get that rig ready and get Ray to town to Doc Slade. And if Ray don't get there in time, you're answering to me . . . plenty!"

Old Joe felt lost and worried five minutes later, as John Ford, Ray beside him, drove his buckboard out of sight upcañon, around a turning in the trail. He climbed up onto the seat and kicked off the brake. He cut the lead team across the ears with his whip, sorry the moment he'd done it. He had never abused his animals.

He settled to the long grind, and the rain turned into a downpour lashed by a cold wind, whipping up a spray off the rocks and trees that made it hard to see the road ahead. It was as miserable a drive as Joe could remember. He was cold to the bone, and, in his sodden discomfort, without Ray's company, he was once more an old man, lonely, without hope, finished.

He had a few regrets, not many. Of course he should have saved his money through the years, put enough aside so that he could spend these last empty years in some degree of comfort, resting. Probably he should have married Martha Drew forty years ago, instead of being afraid to ask her and letting her wait so long she'd finally gone away with Spence Amsden.

But he admitted grudgingly that his good times and his throwing away his money had made up for most of the things he lacked now. When a man couldn't any longer work, he ought to crawl into a hole and pull it in after him.

He thought of John Ford, and of Chet Richter and Barney Ryan. He reached down and took the old Greener from the hangars under the seat and broke open the weapon, seeing that the buckshot loads were fresh. Then he laughed.

"That's one thing you never was, Joe Miles . . . spooky," he growled as he hung the shotgun under the seat again.

He hadn't thought much about the payroll, but, now that he remembered it, he was thinking of the old days when the town up above was booming, when every gold stage carried gun guards inside and out, and even then sometimes didn't get through with their precious freight. That was forty years ago, when the scum of humanity had flocked into these hills with the gold fever, when he'd worn a six-gun, the same as he'd worn his boots, and used it often.

But today wasn't forty years ago. The formality of sending a guard along with each payroll shipment was merely a habit of Len Rivers's, who was of the old school—Joe's school—that had lived the hard way. In case of real trouble, a driver was expected to hand over what was in the boot and let the insurance detectives take care of running down the thieves. Chet Richter and Barney Ryan. Two undersize, lazy tramps who couldn't give a real man a workout either with guns or fists. Men didn't know how to use guns any more, not the way they had forty years ago.

This country was settled, civilized; the stages were giving way to the railroads. Joe Miles and his generation were giving way to men like Ray Dineen and Ted Baker, the new Blue Star superintendent, men who would bring in new and better equipment, run it faster and longer, and make more money, advancing ahead of the railroads and maybe in the end going over to the railroads themselves. In this sober moment, old Joe saw that his being laid off was symbolic of a dying age, and in his loneliness he was a little proud of his past, glad he wasn't just beginning in this new era of change.

The cañon walls fell away and the trail cut in through the low foothills, and in the next two hours old Joe crossed three washes running water, one badly. The rain still held to a steady downpour. He heard the far-off roar of Graveyard Wash from a half mile's distance, and gauged its sound. It was running high; two more hours, he judged, would find it impassable.

His first sight of the wide wash brought a dry chuckle out of his flat chest. Muddy water boiled bank to bank across its hundred-yard width. Already there was better than a foot and a half of water, with three-foot waves churning up over the bars and the sand riffles. There was some driftwood, small seedling trees and bushes that had probably fallen in with caved cut-banks. Soon there would be larger trees. In fact, there was one down already, barely in sight upstream, a half-foot-thick cotton-wood, branches sheered off along its straight trunk, its huge bole of spreading roots turning slowly in cartwheel fashion as it rolled lazily with the force of the current.

He drove as far as the downgrade cutting in the high bank, a pleasing excitement running along his nerves, making him forget how he'd felt back a ways. This was what his life had been, a series of small adventures testing his ingenuity and toughness. Like this, getting two teams and a heavy stage across a roaring torrent. Few men could do it without letting an animal go down or bogging in quicksand. He could; he was still tough enough to do it right.

He pulled in the teams, letting his eye run over harness, the lashings on the boot; he tested the brake, spotted the line of the road opposite, and lifted the reins to send his Morgans into the downgrade.

He heard the cry then, faint yet unmistakable.

"Ray! Ray!"

It was muted by the roar of the water, yet there was an emergency to the voice that brought him to his feet, looking downstream. Then it came again from downstream—"Ray!"—and he was gripped in a paralysis of stark, sudden fear.

It was Sue Dineen's voice.

His bleak old eyes whipped over the angry waters. What he saw made him lift his whip. Twenty rods below, within a quarter of that distance of a sage-studded narrow strip of land still above water toward the far bank, he saw the wagon and the horse and Sue and the kids.

The wagon was bottom side up, the wheels half out of the water. Sue clung to the hub of the near front wheel, only her head and shoulders showing and the water foaming about her shoulders, pressing her in against the wheel. She was caught there; otherwise she'd be with the kids, who were standing above her on the overturned bed of the wagon, only up to their knees in water. One horse was down, drowned, his four stiff legs sticking out of the water. The weight of the carcass must have been dragging at the harness for, as Joe took that one fleeting look, he saw the remaining animal lunge and try to break loose.

With the horse's lunge, Sue screamed. Joe heard it plainly and laid his whip to his teams. As the Concord lurched ahead, tilted into the downgrade, a distant explosion sounded from somewhere behind. Joe looked over his shoulder. A hundred yards back along the trail he saw two riders coming in fast toward him. The one he recognized as Chet Richter aimed a six-gun and fired at him as he watched.

The Concord lurched badly, righted itself, and the Morgans shied down off the bank and into knee-deep water. Old Joe laid on his whip, forgetting that to trot a horse in fast water is unsafe. The off-wheeler stumbled, went to his knees, and was up again. Joe held the horses to a walk, his eye on the wagon downstream. It might have been his imagination, but he thought that Sue was already lower in the water than when he'd first seen her.

All at once, fifty yards out, the right front wheel went down. Too late, old Joe remembered that there was quicksand out here. He whipped the teams and they were pulling clear of the quicksand when suddenly a bronco went down. An instant later the report of a shot cut into the steady roar of the rushing water. Joe looked back to see Chet Richter and Barney Ryan about to head their horses into the water after him. Barney had shot the horse.

The Concord's front wheel sank lower into the quicksand. Then, lazily almost, the stage went over on its side. Joe jumped, landed on the back of the animal alongside the downed bronco, and with his clasp knife he cut the wounded, kicking horse from the tangle of harness. He slid off the back of the animal, stood on the long tongue of the coach. Then, the water boiling about his legs and threatening to drag him off his slender perch, he unhitched the lead team from all but their singletree.

The last thing he did before leaving the overturned Concord was to edge back and cut the lashings from the front boot. He worked feverishly while he watched Barney Ryan and Chet Richter wade their ponies on through the water toward him, Richter brandishing his pistol and calling something unintelligible above the roar of the water. The money chest slid out from the ropes, stuck on a metal brace. Old Joe kicked it viciously and it finally slid into the water with a sucking splash to sink out of sight.

He shook his fist at Ryan and Richter, twenty yards away now and coming forward fast. Then he freed the one remaining wheel bronco with a few deft slashes of his knife and threw himself on the back of one of the leaders. He drove them away from the stage, clear of the tongue, and cut obliquely out at a walk toward the overturned wagon.

He was almost even with it; every muscle in him strained to use the ribbons as a whip; yet he knew it meant disaster and a quick death if the horse he rode lost his footing on the shifting sandy bottom. He looked back once to see Chet Richter sitting his pony alongside the stage, holding Ryan's reins. Ryan was aboard the Concord, kicking in a window, probably in search of the money chest. Old Joe laughed harshly at the thought of how futile their search would be.

Working in toward the wagon now, he called encouragingly: "Steady, Sue! I'm coming."

Then he happened to look upstream. There, less than forty yards away, rolling relentlessly down in line with the wagon, turned the huge bole of the uprooted cottonwood, enough weight in rock and soil in its roots to crush the wagon like matchwood.

"Ray!" Sue called. Then she saw who it was. "Joe! Hurry!" Her voice jerked him out of his momentary paralysis.

Tommy, Ray's ten-year-old boy, was holding onto his sister Ellen. His straight yellow hair, like his Dad's, was plastered down across his forehead. He was crying, calling out in a choking voice to his mother, trying to reach down to take her hand.

The water was up to Sue Dineen's neck, occasionally boiling up over her head so that her call to Joe as he drove the horses alongside was a gasp. "Joe, I'm caught. My legs are under the wagon. Take the children, Joe. Please! Get them away before it's too late."

Joe slid off the back of the horse, holding the reins tight. "Hold on a minute longer!" he called. He darted a glance at the oncoming cottonwood. It was closer, but rolling out of line. There would be time enough now. The water sweeping up his thighs, he waded over and took Ellen under one arm, Tommy under the other.

Tommy fought, screaming—"Don't leave Mother!"—until Joe said: "We'll get her out. Now you act like a man, Tommy." He carried the children back to the horses, and lifted them onto the back of the nearest. "Hold on tight to the belly band!" he shouted, and clamped their hands to the leather. Then he left them for the wagon again.

He was working with an intent coolness now, not wasting a

move. He caught up the one rein of the frantic bay horse still hitched to the wagon. Somehow he backed the animal and then headed him downstream. He gathered the one rein and all at once lashed out fiercely, yelling his lungs out in a high-pitched, sharp yell. The horse, frightened into violent action, lunged against the harness. Joe whipped the animal unmercifully. The wagon slid, turned on its side, and then rolled on downstream as though its weight was no more than a packing box's.

Sue tried to stand, couldn't, and went under. Joe was swept off his knees as he lunged to stop her from being dragged on with the current. He went under, then, miraculously, caught a hold on her skirt and held it.

He struggled to his feet, picked the woman up, and carried her to the horses. She was a dead weight in his arms, limp, but somehow Joe managed to throw her over the back of the horse alongside her children. He slapped her face hard. She stirred and her eyes opened.

He yelled: "Plenty of time now, Sue! Grab a hold and I'll climb on with the kids!" She heard him, pulled herself onto the Morgan's back, and took a hold on the heavy collar, a wave of thankfulness flooding her eyes as she saw that her children were there beside her.

Joe worked on around her horse and in alongside the other. On the way, he saw the cottonwood, its huge bole towering twice as high as his head, ten feet to one side. He was relieved that it had finally rolled out of line with them.

All at once the lower roots tilted crazily. They must have struck a boulder, for the weight of the bole fell outward and whipped the trailing stem of the tree out of the water. It rose from the current in a blinding sheet of spray. The Morgan shied. Old Joe, a weak hold on the harness strap, was dragged off his feet.

The horse lunged, Joe's boots came down into the surging

water, and his hold broke. He fell face down into the muddy, roiling water, his last glance toward the Morgans showing them lunging into a run. Then he was under, rolling over and over along the gravelly bottom. His lungs fought for air, but he held his breath. Then he managed to strike out with hands and knees and slow the force of his rolling weight. The next time he turned over, he was facing squarely downstream, with the current at his back. He struggled to his feet, his head above water and his lungs dragging in pure cold air. He got one full breath before the water swept his legs from beneath him and he was down again.

This time he was under longer, fighting, trying to remember what little he knew of swimming. Once more his head was above water; once more his lungs gasped for air. He struggled to his knees, to his feet. He spread his legs far apart, bracing himself against the mighty suck of the water. He looked downstream. The rolling bole of the cottonwood, trailing its slender trunk, was now nothing but a shadow in the blur of rain, fast disappearing. The horses were out of sight.

He screamed time and again—"Sue! Sue, answer me! Tommy! Ellen!"—but his voice was only a feeble croak in the rush of water and the torrent of the storm.

The strength left his legs and he knew he was going down again, and this time he didn't care. He was too tired to care. He looked dully downstream once more. Coming toward him, dragging the broken front axle and one wheel of the wagon, was the remaining horse of Ray Dineen's team of bays. The horse was plunging wildly, crazed with fear, straight up the stream.

Joe struggled five steps and caught the one trailing rein as the horse lunged by. He held on, dragged hand over hand up the rein until he was alongside the animal. Then, in a last desperate effort, holding to the harness collar, he pulled the horse's head in toward the far bank, his legs dragging along the wash's rocky bottom. The bay stepped on him, tried to kick him, but he was lucky enough to keep his body out of line with the slashing hoofs.

Five minutes later the bay was standing head down on the creekbank, and old Joe was lying on his back in the sand, arms aching.

When he could move, he started walking downstream, looking for some sign of Sue and the children. All he could remember was the plunging horses; the children couldn't have held on. He walked back and forth until dark, and all he found was the blue sweater Ellen had been wearing, caught on the branch of a dead willow two miles below the road. He gave up then, knowing the answer.

He walked back as far as the road and sat on the bank, looking out at the rushing waters through the darkness. There was four feet of water running now, nothing showing of the Concord but one rear wheel idly turning in the current. The rain had stopped. Later, the sky cleared and the stars came out. He walked a half mile, looking for Ray Dineen's bay horse and finally caught him. He found signs along the road that told him Chet Richter and Barney Ryan had ridden back into the hills. He gave them little thought, thinking mostly of Sue and those two kids of Ray's.

At midnight, when he judged he could get the horse across the wash in the receding water, he began to think seriously of what to do. The first thing was to get to Ray, to break the news as gently as he could. He'd tell him how Sue had fought to save the youngsters and then how he'd fought to save them all. He had waited here because the nearest ranch in toward the hills was eight miles away and he was afraid the tired bay couldn't carry him that far. But if he could get the gelding across the wash, there was a homesteader, Caylor, who had a place within a mile.

He cut the one long rein and made two shorter ones of it, fastening them to the bay's bit. He finally climbed onto the bay and headed him into the water, deeper than any he'd ever put a horse into, but he made it.

Caylor's place, a mile down the trail, was deserted. The corral was empty; the wagon Joe had often seen in the barn lot on his way past was gone. So was the homesteader's team. But there was a saddle in the barn, and Joe took the hull and threw it on the bay. He was worried about the tired horse being able to carry him the four miles in to Sands.

The bay horse walked most of the four miles, and during that long hour and a half the ghosts of Sue and Ellen and Tommy Dineen rode with Joe. When he saw the winking lights along the town's street, he felt his first reluctance to face what lay ahead. He'd have to make a report to the sheriff; there would be questions, maybe accusations. He'd have to get the superintendent, young Ted Baker, out of bed and report the loss of four horses and all his equipment.

Of course, they'd find the money chest; the damned money-grubbers would dredge the bed of the wash for ten miles for their payroll. But that wouldn't bring back Sue and Ellen and Tommy Dineen.

He was a quarter of the way along the street when he noticed the scattered crowd along the walk far ahead in front of the lights of the Blue Star stage station. It was late for such a crowd, but then a fight or a noisy drunk or maybe a man hurt could attract these countless loafers who never seemed to sleep.

From far out of the distance came the wailing long note of a locomotive's whistle. Old Joe read a personal insult into the sound. But for the locomotives and the twin ribbons of steel cutting across the plain, he'd still have his job, have it until he died, and Sue and the kids wouldn't have been on their way down today.

He was even with the first stores along the street and riding down toward the group in front of the Blue Star when someone on the walk shouted suddenly: "Look! It's Joe Miles! Either him or his ghost!"

Men stepped down off the walk, looked his way. Then another man shouted—"It ain't no ghost!"—and started running toward him. Half a dozen more followed. The swing doors of a saloon across the street burst outward and a line of men filed out. More came from a saloon farther along and joined the quickly gathering crowd in the street. Someone shouted: "Get him and bring him over here!"

Old Joe didn't know what was happening. He tried to turn the bay, but he wasn't fast enough. Hands reached up and pulled him out of the saddle. He was hoisted to two pairs of shoulders, even though he struck out feebly to shake loose the holds on his legs.

Men crowded those who were carrying him. A few hats went into the air and the shouts grew frenzied. They carried Joe across to the Blue Star stage station. All he knew was that these men were cheering, that they weren't angry. Abruptly he was lowered and pushed up onto the walk to face young Ted Baker, the new Blue Star superintendent, who stood in the office doorway.

Baker held up a hand to command silence. He was smiling as the shouts died away and a stillness settled back along the crowd. Old Joe shook loose a man who was holding him and waited, an ugly twist to his wrinkled face.

"Well, Joe, we hardly know what to say," Ted Baker began.

"You could start by telling me what the hell all this ruckus is about," said Joe. "I don't feel like joking. Something's happened. If you've planned this as a send-off, you young squirt, you can lay off and listen to some bad news. This afternoon I hit Graveyard Wash to find a woman and two kids drowning, Ray Dineen's kids. Trying to get 'em out, I lost your outfit, horses and all. And I lost Sue and the kids, too. Now the whole pack of you clear out and let me. . . ."

"Joe," Baker cut in, "Joe. Sue and the children are across at the hotel, in bed. Alive! Safe! Larry Caylor brought them in, in his wagon. They thought you'd drowned. We all thought you'd drowned. The sheriff has a posse rounded up, ready to start looking for your body at sunup."

Old Joe Miles stood there a good five seconds, while the expectant hush held the crowd. Tears came to his eyes, streamed down his grizzled cheeks. Then, before any of them could reach out to catch him, his knees buckled and he fell full length on the walk in a dead faint.

Ted Baker was more worried than anyone else. For a half hour he paced the hallway before the hotel room where they had carried old Joe. The doctor was in there with Joe, trying to bring him around. The medico was an ornery old devil who insisted on having the room cleared before he went to work.

Finally the door opened.

"What about it?" Ted Baker asked quickly. "Will he live?"

"Live!" the medico snorted. "There's nothing wrong with that old cuss. A little tuckered out, maybe, and bruised a bit. He'll be fit as a fiddle in the morning."

Baker took the chair alongside as Joe sat up. Baker pushed him down again, said: "Take it easy, Joe."

Neither of them said anything for a couple of minutes. Then Baker began: "Sue Dineen told me everything that happened. She thought you'd drowned under that tree. She told me about Chet Richter and Barney Ryan. They were shooting at you, weren't they? They tried to take that payroll, didn't they?"

Joe nodded. "I reckon. But your money's safe in the wash. I wasn't thinking much about Barney and Chet. It was the girl, and them kids. I can't see yet how they got away safe."

Baker shook his head, his glance touched with admiration. "Because of you, Joe." Baker had never before condescended to talk to his driver in this familiar off-hand way. Joe hardly knew what to make of it. "There'll be a reward out for saving that payroll, Joe. It'll amount to maybe five or seven hundred dollars. There's another thing I'd like to talk over."

"Shoot," old Joe said, hoping young Baker wasn't going to go sentimental over his thanks or make more excuses about letting him go.

"It's this, Joe. We've tried Ed Salzman for a year as superintendent on the southern division. He isn't working out well. I've done some thinking. We can run this efficiency and this new system into the ground. What we need is to keep the best of the old-timers, men who can pull us out of a tight spot when we get in one, like the one today. This superintendent's job is mostly inside work, nothing like you're used to. But I was wondering if we could make you decide to stay on a few more years and take it?"

Old Joe swallowed once, trying to clear his throat so he could say yes. Baker understood. He got up out of his chair and went to the door. "I suppose you'll want Ray Dineen for one of your drivers, won't you?"

Joe thought of something, sat up suddenly. "I forgot to tell you about Ray," he said. "This afternoon he. . . ."

"I know," Baker cut in. "A man just rode in with a note from Doc Slade to Ray's wife. Ray had his appendix out. He's in fine shape." He looked at his watch. "Get some sleep and I'll see you in the morning, Joe. We'll whip this line into shape and make it pay."

Old Joe couldn't get to sleep for better than an hour. It didn't worry him much. He had always insisted that a man who slept too much was old or soft, and he wasn't either of these.

★ ★ ★ ★ ★

THREE WHO FLED BOOTHILL

★ ★ ★ ★ ★

This story, titled "The Owl-Hoot Strikes Back", was submitted by Jon Glidden's agent to Mike Tilden at Popular Publications on June 6, 1937. Tilden bought it on October 2, 1937, paying the author $94.50, at the rate of 1 1/2¢ a word. It was published in *Ace-High Magazine* (11/37) as "Three Who Fled Boothill". That title has been retained for its first appearance in book form.

I

He had staked his horse over on the far side of the hill, well out of hearing, and now, a hundred yards below the crest, he paused to take off his boots. When he moved ahead again, slowly, soundlessly, he kept to the cover of the cedars and carried a boot under each arm. He was tall and thin and had a gaunt face, so that his deliberate stealthy stalking made him look ungainly and a little ridiculous.

A moment later he came within sight of his quarry. A man, forty yards below him, lay belly-down on a flat rock ledge, unmoving, his gaze seemingly centered on a cluster of weathered frame buildings far below that hugged the base of the steep slope. At sight of him, Slim's face took on a cunning smile, and he came on even more warily.

Suddenly the man below stirred and rolled quickly onto his back. His two hands came alive and swiveled to the twin holsters at his thighs and streaked up a pair of Colts, lining them at Slim. The whole action took but a second and startled Slim so that his boots slipped from his grasp and thudded to the ground. His mouth gaped open in sheer fright. He swallowed thickly, and called out: "Don't, Mark! It's only me. Swing them cutters away!"

The man called Mark sat up finally and pushed his weapons back into leather. He cursed softly, and with that his lean face lost its bleakness and the tautness went out of his flat, wide frame.

He shook his head soberly, and drawled: "Someday you'll get yourself into a peck of trouble, Slim."

"You're spooky, friend," was Slim's retort as he came on down to sit beside Mark, and pulled his boots back on. "How the hell did you know I was up there? I was moving like a whisper."

He finished with the boots and waited for a reply. When it didn't come, he went on: "Everything's set. I got the whole story in town, like you told me to. Jake drifted in three days ago and went to the bank and paid up your back taxes. They got word to the sheriff some way and he nabbed Jake as he was leaving the bank and took him down to the jail. They say he kept him there for an hour, trying to pump him about where to find you. But Jake kept his mouth shut and sloped out of town that night. It means he's down there at the house now, waiting for us."

Mark's glance shuttled to the spread below once more. The buildings had a run-down look. The poles of the corral were down on one side, and weeds grew in the hard-packed yard in front of the house. "But he isn't down there," Mark said. "There hasn't been sign of a living thing all afternoon."

"There's plenty of talk in town about you," Slim went on, his thoughts uninterrupted by what Mark had told him. "The day after Jake pulled out, a jasper turned up with the news he'd seen you on the Powder Creek trail, heading this way. So the sheriff and a posse spent all day yesterday combing the hills to the west, trying to get a line on where you'd gone. And a gent named Tolliver put up another thousand for you, dead or alive."

"Ralph Tolliver," Mark snapped, his gray eyes widening a trifle in surprise. "I thought Ralph was my friend."

Slim shook his head. "Think again. They say he's the one who was going to buy your outfit if the taxes hadn't been paid. Wants a new home for his bride. He's marrying the sister of the gent you beefed that night. Not that I think you did it, understand, but they. . . ."

Mark's hand streaked out to clamp a vice-like grip on Slim's arm. "Say that again, Slim."

"Ralph Tolliver's marrying the Sanderson girl." Slim pulled his arm away and rubbed it gingerly. "Why, does that change things?"

Mark shook his heard, yet the look in his eyes belied his denial.

"I didn't know," Slim muttered, almost an apology.

They sat in silence then for a long while. Finally Slim got to his feet and looked west toward the low-lying foothills. "You was right, Mark. The town's gone hog-wild. It's full of ore wagons and drummers and gamblers and loose women. Wide open. Four new saloons in the last two weeks. And all because of that." He waved a hand, indicating several new and unpainted shacks that dotted the slopes to the west, toward town. Below each shack was the fan-spread scar of a muck dump. "There's more yellow metal coming out of these hills than any man has seen since Deadwood. And your place here is bound to be worth a mint of money."

"Maybe," said Mark skeptically.

Another silence held them for long minutes. Then it was Slim again who broke it, saying impatiently: "Let's get down to the house. I'd like a square meal for a change. Jake must have stocked up on food, knowing we'd be here today."

"We'll wait until after dark," Mark told him. He looked down at the buildings with a worried frown furrowing his forehead. "I don't like the looks of it, Slim. Not a-tall."

Slim grumbled at this, but sat down again and built himself a cigarette. Abruptly he queried: "What're you back here for, Mark? You know what it'll mean. Nobody knows any better now that you were framed than they did three years ago, when you took out two minutes ahead of that lynch mob. Sanderson was drygulched, and they found your gun alongside his body. That's all they know, and you still ain't going to be able to tell 'em different now."

It was a full ten seconds before he got his answer. "Take a look to the south," Mark said firmly. "See the break off there, where the grass meets the badlands? My range runs all the way to that line. And west, to where that dry wash cuts across from the foothills. Two miles in back of us is my north fence, and the grass runs knee-deep for better than three miles to the east before you hit that border." He paused and turned to Slim, and then concluded: "It's four thousand acres, boy, good acres, and I think it's worth fighting for."

Slim nodded. "I reckon it is. But who are you going to fight?"

"I don't know yet. But I'll never get anywhere riding the dark trails a hundred, two hundred miles away. Maybe if I poke around here a while, I'll bump into something."

"Maybe something'll bump into you," Slim corrected. It was a rare thing for him to hear Mark utter so many words at one time, and to speak so heatedly.

"That's my look-out," Mark grunted. "You and Jake will be safer here than any other place. You're wanted in Idaho. Jake's wanted in New Mexico. Stick with me and we may have the chance to grow old together here at my layout. If that doesn't suit, both of you can ride any time you feel like it."

"It ain't my hide I'm thinking of," Slim complained. "It's yours, partner. I'd hate to see that bounty paid on you."

"I'll do the worrying."

That concluded their discussion. They watched the sun's red disk slip below the far, flat horizon and tinge the snow fields on the peaks to the right a coral hue, broken here and there by the bright emerald of some high hill pasture. Mark's eyes were chiefly for the layout below; he looked down at it as though fascinated, as if in seeing it once again he was satisfying some age-long hunger. Yet his frown deepened as the quick dusk settled and hid the buildings in shadow. He was worried at not seeing any sign of Jake, who should have been waiting for them.

Finally, when the full darkness had come on, he said: "We'll give it a try now."

II

The descent was steep. Because they chose to move quietly, they took a full half hour to reach the valley floor. They approached the layout from the corral side, and, as the shadowed skeleton of the enclosure came up out of the darkness, Mark took Slim by the arm, pulled him close, and said in a low voice: "The house is straight ahead. In five minutes you head for it with your gun out. I'm circling to come in from the front. If Jake was there, we'd have seen him long before this."

He was gone into the night before Slim could give an answer. This was old, familiar ground, and Mark circled to the front of the house with the certainty of a man who knows well what he is doing. Once there, among the cottonwoods that edged the wide yard, he paused long enough to lift the six-gun from his right holster.

He was within ten yards of the house when he saw the dim outline of a man's bulky form edge suddenly around the near corner.

"Jake?" he called softly.

He had his reply in a thundering, flame-lancing gun blast. It lit the darkness for a split second to show him an unfamiliar face peering intently across at him. With that flash of light came a slamming blow at his left shoulder. It spun him part way around and threw him off-balance. He dug his heels into the solid ground and brought his gun around and thumbed an answering shot. And then he heard Slim's shouting from behind, and caught sight of his friend running across the yard toward him.

He was about to voice a warning to Slim when he saw the man's outline ahead of him lurch forward and sprawl to the ground. Slim came up an instant later, muttered an oath, and kneeled beside the prostrate form. Mark saw him reach out and wrench the gun from the man's outstretched, lifeless hand, and then heard him call out: "You hurt?"

"Take care of him while I have a look inside," was Mark's answer. He was reassured by the absence of any other unfamiliar sound. It took him five seconds to reach the back door of the house and to try the knob, and to find it locked. With one thrusting kick he broke open the door and stepped quickly inside. The darkness was unrelieved here, and for a moment Mark stood debating what to do next. Then he remembered a trick his father had taught him, and reached into the pocket of his shirt and brought out a match.

His left shoulder was stiff and aching. He found that out when he changed his heavy .45 from right hand to left. But he could use the hand, and he held the gun steadily before him and palmed the match in his right hand, then hurled it far out, across the floor.

In the sudden flare he made out a figure in a chair across the room and instantly recognized Jake. He crossed over and quickly pulled the gag out of Jake's mouth. "The gent I just plugged outside . . . the only one around?" he asked brusquely.

"He's the only one," was Jake's croaking answer. "Get these ropes off me, will you?"

Reassured, Mark struck another match and lit the lamp he found on the table alongside the door. As the yellow flush of the lamp glow cut the gloom, he returned to his friend. Jake's thick-set frame was tied securely in a straight-backed chair. The livid line of a bruise ran across his forehead, while above it showed a smear of hair-matted blood.

Mark took out his knife and cut Jake loose. It took all his strength, for now his shoulder throbbed in pain and his sleeve was wet with blood. He turned away so that Jake wouldn't see and asked in a level voice: "What happened?"

Jake got stiffly out of his chair and staggered across to the table and lifted a dipper full of water from the pail standing there. He emptied the dipper in three hasty gulps.

Suddenly Jake heard a soft thud behind him and turned in time to see Mark roll over onto his back, his face shades lighter than its usual tan.

"Slim!" he bellowed in alarm. "Get in here!"

Then, hearing Slim's steps come pounding around the far end of the cabin, Jake dipped more water and threw it in Mark's face. Mark stirred, groaned softly, and opened his eyes.

Slim rushed in at the door, his six-gun in his fist. He saw at a glance what had happened, and pushed Jake roughly to one side. "Anyone who'd give us the kind of a greeting you did ought to be wearing knee pants, brother," he growled.

"Step aside and let me handle this."

Mark tried to sit up, but Slim pushed down again and ripped off his sleeve so that he could see the wound. "This calls for a sawbones," he said. "Stay where you are and we'll bring in the lad you plugged outside and make it a hospital." He took off his bandanna, bound it around Mark's shoulder, and then said to Jake: "Let's fetch your friend."

Slim rose and led the way out. After a brief interval he and Jake reappeared, carrying between them the limp form of the man Mark had wounded. "He's got a thick head," Slim told Mark. "I'm sorry to say I think he may live."

At that moment, as the light from the lamp fell across the wounded man's face, Mark gave a gasp of surprise. "Harl Brender! Why was he here, Jake?"

"You know him?" Jake queried disapprovingly. "He can't be your friend. Last night he was waiting at the corral as I rode in. Gave me a pistol-whipping before I knew what hit me. And today he kept me laced in that chair, laughing every time I asked him for a drink. I reckon he thought he'd get it out of me where to find you."

"He always was forked," Mark said. "Three years ago he was rodding the Whiplash outfit, over east. Later I heard that the bank foreclosed on the layout. Wonder why he's trying to mix in this?"

"You can wait for your answer," Slim told him, a worried frown on his face as he saw that his simple bandage had not stopped the flow of blood from Mark's shoulder. He turned to Jake. "You get some water boiling on the stove and find a clean towel and put it in that hole in his shoulder. I'm heading for town."

It did no good for Mark to protest. Five minutes later Slim pounded out from the corral astride Jake's chestnut mare. Mark had told him to get Doc Swain, and he had also cautioned: "The old fool may not want to come. If he gets stubborn, stick a gun in his ribs and tell him Mark Healy's in trouble."

III

Cornelius Swain, known to his best friends as Cornie and to casual acquaintances as Doc, was plainly worried. He sat on the bed in Ralph Tolliver's sparsely furnished hotel room and slowly turned the chewed butt of a cigar over and over between his thin lips. His slit-eyed glance was now focused on the man sitting in the chair across the room.

"It was a damned fool play, Tolliver," he snapped. "We'll lose our shirts tonight if that stage doesn't get through."

Ralph Tolliver shifted uncomfortably and tilted his chair back against the wall. He was young and handsome, his face long and aquiline with a hint of weakness to the chin, but the hardness of his pale blue eyes took that weakness away. He made a striking figure, outfitted fashionably in gray frock coat, white shirt, string tie, and low-heeled, fancy-stitched boots.

"No one will lose anything," he said, his tone suave and unruffled. "It was the only thing to do, Doc."

"The hell it was," Swain snorted. "You got a two-ton safe in your store. All this talk about hardcases busting in and carrying that gold off is drivel. Instead of leaving it there for the two weeks until the new bank is finished, you make us load the sixty thousand onto a stage and run it down to Glenwood, with a damn' good chance of losing the whole shipment."

"Only four of us know what the stage is carrying, Doc," Tolliver said. "In two hours more it'll be safe in the vaults at Glenwood. I tell you, I didn't want the responsibility of having it in my store. Besides, our bank won't be finished in two weeks, maybe not in two months. You can't hire men to lay brick here now. They're all up in the hills at the diggings."

"What if someone should hold up the stage?" Doc asked savagely.

"It's more likely they'd rob the safe in the store. Remember, Doc, Mark Healy and his wild bunch are on the loose around here."

Doc snorted his disgust and got up off the bed and crossed to the door, still chewing his cigar. There he turned and said levelly: "I'd expect to hear that from you, Ralph. You know damn' well Mark Healy's no robber. And you know we ran a chance sending that gold down tonight. You could stand to lose your share and not miss it. I couldn't. Neither could a lot of others. Sanderson's one. He needs his gold to pay off the mortgage on the hotel here." He paused a moment, and a cunning light edged into his glance as he went on: "Are you really marrying Sanderson's girl, Ralph, or is she changing her mind now that they've hit that nice little vein up on their claim?"

Ralph Tolliver came up out of his chair in one lithe, quick surge of motion. In three steps he crossed the room to stand facing the medico. Swain stood his ground. "See here, sawbones," Tolliver breathed, his tone holding a strident menace. "Don't let that talk get around. Gail Sanderson loves me and that's why we're getting married."

"That so?" Doc said, unafraid, his shaggy brows rising in polite inquiry. "I'm glad I found that out. You see, I had the idea Gail kind of liked Mark Healy. Well, well," he went on, giving Tolliver no chance to interrupt. "That shows how wrong a man can be. I sure hope it's a good match. You've got my good wishes, Ralph."

He stretched out his hand in a devilishly affable gesture that caught the other off guard. Tolliver took the hand and mumbled an awkward—"Thanks."—knowing as he did it that Swain had made his point. Yet he couldn't overlook one thing, and hastened to add: "You're all wrong about Gail and Mark Healy, Doc. After all, he killed Joe Sanderson. How could she still like him?"

Doc shrugged and said silkily: "Of course she couldn't. Forget I mentioned it." He turned and went out the door and closed it behind him.

On his way down the stairs to the lobby there was a satisfied twinkle in his rheumy old eyes. Swain had reached the paunchy age; he was thirty pounds heavier than five years ago and he moved deliberately these days. He came down the stairs slowly, his glance searching out a girl who stood behind the small desk in the lobby.

This was Gail Sanderson, who helped her father at the desk evenings now that the town was crowded and every room in the hotel filled. She smiled as she saw Swain coming toward her.

"You folks are sure on easy street now," he said, pausing at the desk. "Maybe you'll be building an addition to the place this winter?"

"You're joking, Cornie," Gail answered. Her strong, pretty face took on a more serious expression then, and a troubled look crept into her brown eyes as she asked in a low voice: "Do you think the stage will get through all right?"

"It will if Mark Healy and his gang don't stick it up," Doc said. His face had taken on a set inscrutability as he studied the girl's reaction to this sudden thrust.

Her face colored deeply, and an angry light flared into her glance. "Doc!" she said, addressing him by his more formal name. "How can you say a thing like that? Mark Healy would never steal."

Swain's face took on a relieved smile. "I know he wouldn't," he hastened to say. Then he added: "That's what I told Tolliver. He said some awful things about Mark."

Again he saw that anger edge into her glance. But this time it was different. She was proudly defiant now, in a way that made her very beautiful, and she said: "Ralph Tolliver and I don't agree on a few things. That's one of them."

Swain chuckled softly and told her: "Keep thinking that way about Mark, girl. You're liable to see him again one of these days." And with that he sauntered out the door, leaving Gail with a half-embarrassed yet pleased tide of color mounting to her cheeks.

Swain whistled on the way to his office, which lay beyond the crowded business district. He avoided this part of town lately, hating the things that had changed its main street from a placid narrow lane to a moiling, crowded thoroughfare. There was some consolation in the fact that his small claim was paying him big dividends in the short hours he could spare to work it, yet Doc had never had need of money and he would gladly have done without it to bring back the old, quiet days.

He turned in at the walk that led to his small house, climbed the porch steps, and opened the door, grumbling at his careless-ness in having forgotten to turn out his lamp. Then he saw the tall man standing there with a leveled six-gun in his hand and he pushed the door shut behind him and said calmly: "What kind of a 'howdy' is that, stranger?"

Slim jerked the snout of his weapon to one side to indicate the cabinet full of shining instruments that stood against the far wall, drawling flatly: "Gather up your things and come with me, Doc. There's a man hurt bad."

Swain's glance became quizzical, almost polite. He chose to ignore the menacing gun and said: "Anyone I know?"

"Grab your bag and lay off the questions," was Slim's brusque rejoinder. He was nervous tonight, worried about Mark, and his temper was short. "You'll see who it is quick enough. I saddled your jughead. He's waiting out back with mine."

Swain crossed to his desk and got his black bag. Then he looked pointedly at Slim's gun and said: "Is it necessary for you to keep that thing in your hand, friend?"

Slim said—"No, I reckon it ain't."—and dropped his weapon into the holster at his thigh. Doc nodded and turned to the glass-fronted case behind him and opened the door and took out several instruments. Then he came back to the desk and opened his case and put the instruments into it. When his hand came out again, it held a short, double-barreled Derringer.

"Now talk," he breathed. "Tell me who it is and where you're taking me. I might want to drop you off at the jail before mak-ing my call."

Slim gulped in amazement and his hand started to reach down for his gun. But at that moment he distinctly heard the hammer click of the Derringer as Swain cocked it. He hesitated, and then managed to get out: "We wouldn't hurt you, Doc. It's one gent with a hole through his shoulder and another with a busted head. You see they got into an argument and. . . ."

"Who are they? Where are they?" Swain snapped out, his weapon still centered on Slim's belt buckle.

Slim hesitated in answering, his jaw suddenly cording in stubborn resolve to keep his secret. But Swain's unblinking gaze and the threat of that wicked little Derringer were too much. "It's Mark Healy," Slim blurted out. "He's hurt bad with a slug in his shoulder. The other's. . . ."

"Who gives a damn about the other one!" Swain roared. "Why didn't you tell me it was Mark?" He dropped the Derringer into his bag, snapped it shut, and came from behind his desk in a hurry. "Well, what're you waiting for, High Pockets? Let's be going!"

Slim swallowed his amazement and led the way out back, to where two horses stood tied to the top pole of Swain's small corral. They got up into their saddles and Slim led the way. But soon Doc put his horse into a swinging run that took him past Slim, and from there on the tall one had all he could do to keep the sawbones in sight.

The brevity of Doc Swain's greeting had been eloquent. A warm light had softened his glance as he crossed the room to take Mark's hand in a firm, sure grasp. "This does me good, Mark," he had said. And then, without one wasted motion, he had dressed Mark's wound, mumbling gruffly as he finished: "Nothing but a hole. No bones broken, and it's clean. Show me this other gent."

He had paid scant attention to the unmoving figure on the floor in the darkened corner of the room. But now he stepped over and looked down at the man, and the other three distinctly heard his quickly indrawn breath. "Harl Brender," he gasped, and then whirled quickly to face Mark. "What's Harl doing here?"

Mark told him, briefly, and ended by saying: "Maybe you can

help us, Cornie. Why would Harl be forted up here, waiting his chance to get me?"

"It's Tolliver," Swain muttered, cursing softly with a pent-up rage that surprised the others. "Harl's still with his old outfit, the Whiplash. But now it belongs to Ralph Tolliver. Ralph bought up the mortgage from the bank when they foreclosed. It was him that started this rush for gold. He found the yellow metal up in the hills on the Whiplash range. He and Harl are as thick as blood brothers. This looks bad, Mark."

"Meaning that it's Tolliver who's after my scalp?"

"Just that. Tolliver must have had a hunch you'd head for the home place after you'd been seen up the Powder Creek trail the other day. Nothing would please him better than to collect his own bounty on you. It's Gail that's got him worried, Mark. She still thinks a lot of you."

Mark was silent for a moment, a new, strange light coming into his eyes. And in the awkward silence that followed each one of them was busy with his own thoughts, trying to digest this unlooked-for news. Harl Brender lay without moving, breathing thickly, his round, ugly face a sickly yellow under the lamplight.

It was Swain who broke the silence to say: "There's only one way of ever finding out what's behind this. Harl's been out cold since your bullet creased his scalp. He may be out for another six hours, or he may come to any minute now. He isn't hurt bad, but that bullet gave his brain a terrific wallop. Slight concussion, I'd call it." He kneeled to examine Brender's wound more closely. At length he straightened up and looked at Mark and went on: "Harl won't know what's happened to him. He probably doesn't even know who he shot at out there in the dark. You gents had better lay him back out there, put his gun in his hand, and let him wake up when he feels like it and try and guess what's happened. I won't even put a bandage on his head. The wound's clean and the air'll do it good."

"And what about us?" Mark said. "I came back here to prove I didn't beef Joe Sanderson, Cornie. And I'm not leaving until I do."

Swain was thoughtful a moment. "It's a cinch you can't stay here," he declared. Abruptly he looked up and said: "I've got it. The three of you can hole up in my shack at the claim. Tomorrow I'll drive up there in the buggy and bring you some grub. Maybe some news. Now let's get this whippoorwill moved out of here before he comes out of it."

IV

Swain was impatient to get back to town. Strangely enough, his first thought had been that he would have to share his secret with Gail Sanderson. But as he weighed this idea more soberly, he knew that the happiness it would give her to know about Mark might in the end become bitterness. *Better wait until he's in the clear,* he told himself.

As he was coming in from the stable, he heard the rumble of iron-tired wheels pounding up the trail toward the edge of town. Seconds later he saw a lumbering stagecoach pass down the darkened street out front and instantly recognized it as the one that had started for Glenwood earlier that evening.

What're they doing back so soon? he asked himself, and went around the corner of his house and onto the street. Looking down its narrow length, he saw that the stage had pulled up in front of Tolliver's hardware store, far up the street, and that a crowd was forming around it. A sudden foreboding told Swain that there had been trouble.

Once inside the store he caught Ralph Tolliver's eye and went with him behind one of the counters, out of hearing of the others. "What happened?" he asked.

Tolliver's handsome countenance wore a worried frown. "Hold-up," was his terse answer. "Mark Healy and his wild bunch. Britt Hardy and the others fought 'em off but didn't think it was safe to go on. So they turned around and brought the stage back. Hell, Doc, this means serious trouble. What did I tell you about . . . ?"

Tolliver broke off as he looked toward the front doors and saw Gail Sanderson step into the long room. The next moment she spied them, and as she approached her eyes blazed defiantly. She came to stand directly before Tolliver, and to ask him levelly: "Are you going out there and stop that talk about Mark, Ralph?"

Tolliver cleared his throat nervously and replied: "How can I? Britt was driving and had a good look at Mark. I can't deny something that's true. They'd laugh at me."

"Britt Hardy didn't see Mark Healy," Gail said, her voice rising. "Mark would never steal. Britt lied."

Tolliver flushed at this, yet he covered his confusion quickly and lifted his shoulders in a gesture of helplessness. Seeing that, Gail turned to Swain: "You know this isn't true. Why don't you do something about it?"

Knowing what he did, Doc Swain had a hard time disguising his feelings. It hurt him to tell her: "Gail, no amount of words can fix this now. Go on over to the hotel and get a good sleep and forget about it if you can. Tomorrow, we'll see what we can do."

The girl stared at her friend in disbelief. Swain had refused to defend Mark Healy for the first time, and it stunned Gail to realize it. Her look of defiance gradually gave way to one of wonder. Once she started to speak, then checked her words and turned away and went out onto the street.

Swain's glance followed her, and as she disappeared through the doors he muttered: "This is going to be hard on her." Then, remembering Tolliver's presence, he added: "Take it easy with her, Ralph. She'll get over it, and then you'll have your chance."

He sauntered out from behind the counter and followed the girl. The store owner's face took on the hint of a smile as he watched the doctor's retreating back. He hadn't hoped to convince those two so easily, particularly Swain.

Half an hour later Tolliver locked the store and went across to the hotel. The desk in the lobby was deserted as he went in and climbed the stairs to his room. A satisfied smile took control of his features once his door was closed.

He wasn't ready to sleep yet, so he lit a cigar and sat down in the rocker alongside his bed, calmly cataloguing the incidents of the evening. Britt Hardy had given a pretty persuasive account of the attempted hold-up. He'd even shown the crowd three bullet holes through the back of his driver's seat.

Tolliver's cigar had become a three-inch butt when the knock sounded at his door. It brought him out of his chair in a hurried lunge. Then he smiled thinly at his nervousness and reached over to turn down the lamp. He took a short-barreled .38 from his shoulder holster and held it in his left hand as he inched open the door and looked out into the dimly lit hall.

It was Harl Brender. Tolliver swung the door open, and, seeing the crude bandage showing from under the man's Stetson, growled irritably: "Get in." When Brender had entered, Tolliver closed the door behind him, gave his hireling a scornful look, and said: "Let's have it."

Brender swallowed with difficulty, seeing the look in Tolliver's eye. "He got away," he muttered submissively.

Brender had expected an outburst, but not what came. For Tolliver's blue eyes smeared over in a look of open rage and he said: "At times I think I could get along without you, Harl. This is one of the times."

Brender's blanched face lost another shade. "How the hell could I help it?" he flared. But Tolliver's glance quickly killed his belligerence and he went on more mildly: "I did the best I could, boss. I swear it. I found that jasper we spotted in town the other day and had him hog-tied and gagged in the house out there tonight when this Mark Healy came driftin' in. I let him have it, not twenty feet off, and I saw my slug take him. But some damn' fool luck let him get in a shot at me. It did this." He took off his Stetson and ripped his bandanna away and showed Tolliver the open wound on his scalp. "I was out for three hours. When I come to, there wasn't a livin' soul around."

Tolliver paced up and down the short length of his room, and Harl Brender's color, meanwhile, was not improving. He watched Tolliver with a harried, hawk-like glance, and as the moments dragged by he let his hand edge to within finger span of his six-gun. Finally Tolliver stopped his pacing and turned to Brender and saw the man's uncertain, wary gesture. He laughed softly and said: "You'd never get away with it, Harl. Once I'm dead the rest of you stand a good chance of swinging from a rope. There's a bunch of papers over in my safe that'll put every lawman in Arizona on your trail. Yours, and Britt's."

He paused, watching the effect of the words on Brender, whose hand came away from his gun and opened and closed nervously. "That's better," Tolliver murmured, chuckling softly. Abruptly his face went serious again and he continued: "I'll forget what you did tonight, Harl. Only don't slip the next time. Tomorrow night that stage heads for Glenwood with the gold again. Britt will be driving. You and Jerry and Tip will be waiting at Miller's Ford. This time I want it played right. That's all."

"Sure, boss," Harl said, immediately relieved. "I won't never do this wrong. . . ."

"That's all," Tolliver cut in. "You can go now."

Brender meekly turned and went to the door. There he hesitated, about to say something, but in the end he thought better of it, opened the door, and quietly disappeared into the dark hallway.

V

It was dusk when Doc Swain drove his buggy up to his shack at the diggings above town the next evening. A close observer would have wondered at the Doc's unloading so many supplies from the compartment behind the buggy's seat. But up here men sweat at their own work with feverish activity and had little time for other people's business, so that Doc carried his bundles into the shack without arousing any suspicion. Once the task was finished, he closed the door, drew the burlap sacking across the windows, and lit the lamp on the small slab table.

"That's better," Slim said, once the lamplight cut the shadows. "I was thinking we'd have to fumble around in the dark."

Swain took a look at Mark's shoulder, pronounced it better, and then helped Slim cook the meal. As they finished eating, Swain began his story of the happenings of the previous night, and Mark and Slim and Jake listened without once interrupting. When the doctor had finished, Mark took out his tobacco and papers and rolled a cigarette, using his left hand a little awkwardly because of the sling.

"So Tolliver won't let you keep the gold in his safe another day," Mark mused. "And Britt is driving tonight again and another of Tolliver's men is riding guard along with a man that Sanderson's sending along. And everyone in the country knows the stage is making the trip, which means that Mark Healy could get the word and make sure this time. Am I right, Cornie?"

"Right as hell. And there's not one damned thing we can do about it."

"There is something we can do about it," Mark drawled. Then, before Swain could interrupt: "The trail is fairly open for a mile out of town before she cuts down into the cañon. That's too close to town for anything to happen. Then for six and a half miles there isn't room enough to stand a burro alongside a stage hogging the right of way. But at Miller's Ford there's a quarter mile straightaway with room on both sides. It'll happen right there, Cornie."

"Sure," Swain snapped. "I've got it figured that far. They'll probably beef Stebbins, the gent Sanderson is sending along as shotgun guard, first thing. Britt Hardy and the others will come dragging home toward morning, without their guns, and maybe with a few busted heads and some bruises, and we'll hear of how they fought and got licked and had to fork over the gold in the end. And that's all there'll be to it. Sanderson and I and all the rest lose every ounce of dust we've got to our names. And if we accuse Tolliver of the thing before it comes off, he can laugh at us and make us look like fools. He's got the town by the tail."

"Couldn't four good men stop Tolliver's play?" Mark asked quietly.

Swain's head jerked up, and his eyes narrowed as he caught the meaning behind Mark's words. "Meaning me for the fourth?" He paused, considering. Then he got deliberately to his feet and said: "I've got a saddle in the shed out back. What're we waiting for?"

Britt Hardy let the reins go slack in his hands as the two teams took to the water, splashed across the ford, and climbed the steep bank on the other side. He turned his head and glanced at Stebbins, who was riding the back boot, and then muttered to the man beside him: "Let him have it."

His companion faced around, raised his shotgun, and pulled both triggers. In the flare of that double concussion, Stebbins's burly form jerked spasmodically, and he came to his feet screaming in pain. Then he doubled up and fell off the back of the coach to hit the ground hard and lie without moving a muscle.

"Nice work," commented Britt. "Harl and the boys are waiting in the trees up ahead." Hardly had he finished speaking when three horsemen came out of the shadowed margins of the cedar belt that flanked the trail ahead. Britt recognized Brender, Jerry Hawkins, and Tip Ruling.

But at that moment a rifle cracked ominously from the nearer margins of the trees, and the man beside Britt dropped his shotgun and clawed at his chest and fell sideways into Britt. Harl and his two companions wheeled their horses at the sound of the shot, and when the next brittle *crack* sounded, their six-guns blasted back an answering staccato.

Mark was the first to leave the cover of the cedars. He was bent low on the off-side of the saddle and his gelding streaked toward Harl and his two companions at a weaving run. In three seconds he was within range, and then his .45 spoke twice. Harl Brender sloped out of his saddle and hit the ground in a sprawling dive, with his right leg dragging, stiff and useless, behind him.

Slim followed Mark, riding in close and then throwing himself from the saddle to take shelter behind a huge boulder. Slim's first shot sent Britt Hardy down off the seat in frantic haste, to take cover behind his drag team.

Now Britt was emptying his gun at the boulder. Then he was frantically shucking empty shells out of his weapon as Doc Swain galloped up, circled, and brought him into view, throwing one flame-lancing shot at him. Britt snapped out of his crouch, an agonized scream breaking from his lips. He staggered toward Swain, and then abruptly fell face down, unmoving.

It was over in one brief half minute. Harl's two companions, seeing their leader down, threw away their guns and lifted their hands. Jake had been waiting ahead in the trail, ready to cut off any attempt at escape. Now he rode in, dismounted, and walked over to look down at Harl Bender. Something he saw made him kneel quickly and call out.

"Get over here quick, Doc!"

Brender opened his eyes a moment later and looked up at Jake, croaking hoarsely: "Water. Get me some water."

Mark had a sudden thought that made him take Swain by the arm and lead him to one side as Jake went to the creek.

"We're just where we were last night," Mark said, his voice barely above a whisper. "We can't hang this on Ralph Tolliver yet. He can say his men sold him out, did the job on their own. Would a little plain lying to a dying man hurt any, Cornie?"

Swain shook his head. "Not if it gets us what we want."

"Then don't let Brender see you," Mark put in hastily. "It might spoil my play." Before Doc could get his meaning, he had sauntered over to stand alongside the wounded man again.

Brender looked up and recognized Mark with a show of surprise. "You . . . you're Healy," he said, his voice barely above a whisper. "I thought. . . ."

"Ralph sold you out," Mark told him levelly. "There's only three of us, meaning a bigger split for him. He wanted to get rid of you anyway, Harl, after the way you slipped up on that job last night." Mark gave the lie calmly, and waited.

His words brought a visible change to Harl Brender's face. A moment ago all that had showed there was pain and fear. But now, as he took in what he had heard, his features twisted into ugliness. "You're lying, Healy," he said without conviction.

Mark lifted his shoulders in a careless shrug. "Why should I have to lie? You're done for. Tolliver's rid of you."

"He'd never hire the man he framed," Harl choked out, blood flecking his lips. "He'd never. . . ." He broke off in a gasping breath.

"He did, though," Mark said, pressing his point. "I'm to get an extra five hundred for putting you out of the way. What's this about him framing someone?"

"You," Harl whispered, a sudden flow of energy giving him the strength to speak. "He'll do the same with you as he's done to me. Watch out for that sidewinder, Healy. He framed you before and he'll . . . he . . . he was the one who gut-shot Joe Sanderson. Your gun . . . the one they found beside Sanderson . . . Ralph paid me to steal it from your saddlebag that night. Afterward . . . when you went away . . . I. . . ."

Brender's body suddenly went limp. Jake leaned over and felt of his wrist and stood up once again and slowly shook his head. Harl Brender was dead.

Mark looked over at Doc Swain and said softly: "You're a witness, Cornie. That's all I needed." Then he turned to Jake and said tersely: "You'll take the stage on into Glenwood, Jake. Slim can herd these other two back to town." And with that he walked to his horse and swung into the saddle and started back up the trail.

Slim growled something unintelligible and started to follow, but Swain stopped him. "Don't, High Pockets. If he buys trouble, I'd better be the one to help."

The doctor walked over to his horse and mounted and set out after Mark at a stiff run. Slim watched until the doctor had disappeared, and then took off his Stetson and hurled it to the ground at his feet: "And we're left standing here! After coming all this way!" Then he looked over at Harl Brender's two companions and drawled: "For two *pesos* I'd plant some lead in your skulls and go along with those two. How about it, Jake?"

Jake shook his head: "We'd be in the way. Doc knows what he's doing. Come on, let's get this over with."

Ten minutes later they were headed down the cañon, Jake at the stage's ribbons, Slim leading the way with the two bandits tied into their saddles.

Ralph Tolliver leaned on the hotel counter and tried for the third time to get a response from Gail Sanderson: "It wasn't me that did it, Gail. Britt Hardy swore he saw Mark."

Gail sat behind the small table at the rear of the counter. Just now she looked up at Tolliver and said icily: "I've told you I don't care to discuss Mark. And if you know. . . ." Her glance, running beyond Tolliver, took in Mark Healy's entrance, and her surprised gasp at what she saw warned Ralph, who turned slowly to face the door. Mark had stepped inside, and Swain stood two paces behind him.

"Harl Brender died a half hour ago," Mark said, his gaze riveted on the store owner. "He talked before he cashed in."

Tolliver's face lightened a shade in color. To cover his confusion, he snapped out: "There's three thousand on your head, Healy. Are you asking someone to collect it?"

"I am," Mark said flatly. "Only you're wrong about it being three thousand on my head. It's on yours now. Harl told us how he got my gun that night, how you killed Joe Sanderson, and how you framed it on me. Your time's up, Tolliver."

Swain stepped beside Mark and put in: "He's right, Ralph. I heard every word. You'd better come along and see the sheriff and do your talking to him."

Tolliver's face took on a cunning smile. "I'll do that," he drawled. "It shouldn't be hard to make the sheriff listen to reason." His right hand raised to his coat lapel, and Mark, seeing that, let his hand fall to the butt of his Colt.

But Tolliver's hand dipped under his lapel and came out holding his big brown leather cigar case. He leisurely took out a cigar, bit off the end, and reached up to return the case to his inside pocket. The gesture nearly caught Mark unawares, but at the last split second he saw Tolliver's hand sweep up from his pocket. And in that instant Mark's right hand was blurring to his gun.

Tolliver had the advantage by a shade. He wrenched his gun out of the shoulder holster and brought it swinging down as Mark's weapon cleared leather. Then Mark was lunging to one side as Tolliver's .45 cut loose its deafening blast. Mark's tall frame flinched at the impact of the bullet low on his right side. An instant later his thumb had slipped off the hammer of his gun and its roar prolonged that of Tolliver's.

Ralph Tolliver straightened rigidly, as though suddenly paralyzed. His face twisted horribly and he dropped his six-gun and clutched at his throat with clawed fingers. Blood from a blue spot at his throat crept out between his fingers. He opened his mouth to speak but no sound came. And then, as Mark lowered his gun, Tolliver's solid frame tottered and he took a half step that threw him off-balance. Abruptly his knees gave way and he sank to the floor, the force of his fall carrying him onto his back so that his two eyes stared upward glassily.

Gail Sanderson's sobbing cry cut the momentary stillness. "You're hurt, Mark," she choked out, coming quickly from behind the counter.

He stretched out a hand and stopped her: "It isn't much," he said reassuringly. And with that, an infinite tenderness edged out the fear that had shown in her eyes. Abruptly Mark's right arm went out to her and she came to him and raised her face for his kiss.

Swain kneeled beside Tolliver. "Cleanest shot I ever saw," he muttered, looking up at the pair standing nearby. But they paid him no attention, so he took off his coat and covered Ralph Tolliver's face with it. As he got to his feet, his face took on its first genuine smile in more than two days.

★ ★ ★ ★ ★

THE COWBOY
AND THE NESTER

★ ★ ★ ★ ★

The author's original title for this story was "The Cowboy and the Nester". It was submitted to Mike Tilden at Popular Publications who bought it on October 30, 1947. Jon Glidden was paid $360 at the word rate of 3¢. The title of the story was changed to "Hell's Free for Nesters!" when it appeared in *Dime Western* (4/48). For its appearance here the original title has been restored.

I

It was a sorry sight, except for the girl. The wagon's end gate was under and the muddy brown current coiled around and over it as it would momentarily lift a little, then settle back again. The girl was using the whip, not well, and the ox on the off-side would take the punishment matter-of-factly, his movements sluggish and deliberate and never quite matching the lunging effort of the Grulla mare, his harness mate. So it was a see-saw affair, accomplishing nothing beyond working the rear wheels deeper into the sand.

Bill Wells decided it must be another nester wagon headed for Rifle and on to one of the homesteads up along the Squaw Creek range. They'd been coming through for a week now, drawn by Ted Markus's fanciful summons, and would probably keep coming for another month—a tribe of regular down-at-the-heel farmers with their worn-out gear, everything they owned, loaded into the wagons and usually a milk cow or two trailing along behind and a litter of dirty kids sometimes walking or sometimes riding the wagon or even riding the cows.

Bill guessed that maybe his having watched them roll along the road that crossed the bottom of the meadow back where he'd worked was one of the reasons he was moving on. There were other reasons, of course. One was the same fiddle-footedness that had brought him wandering all the way up here from New Mexico Territory last summer just to have a look at some new country. Another was that he'd laid by a good stake over the winter and early spring. Yesterday he'd got to thinking he was a fool, still working when he had already saved as much as a man could rightly want or need. So along about noon he had drawn his wages, tied his possibles in the blanket roll, and ridden away from a good job. It was nice to be on his lonesome again with no one to answer to, nice to be headed for a lot of country that wasn't yet fenced or plowed or cluttered in any way. And he hadn't gone nearly far enough yet, as this bogged-down wagon was showing him.

He wouldn't have bothered stopping if he'd seen any menfolk around. But the only person he could spot was this girl and, nester or not, he couldn't pass her by. So now he reined the chestnut on across the ford marked by two blazed cedar posts on either bank. Once the water came belly-deep to the gelding, he lifted his long legs from the stirrups and crossed his boots ahead of the horn, saying gently—"Steady, Red, steady."—to help the animal. Then when he struck the shallows, he swung on down toward the wagon.

When the girl finally saw him coming, he noticed the way she settled back on the high seat, the straightness going from her spine and the reins hanging loosely. He had known she was young when he had first seen her from a distance, for she had a certain slimness about her that couldn't have belonged to a skinny, older woman. As he drew closer, the oval of her face under the sunbonnet gradually bore out the promise her figure had made from a distance. Her plain gray flannel dress was tightly gathered at the waist and the gentle roundness above that slender line was a youthful and utterly feminine contour. And as she reached up just now and swept the bonnet back off her head, looking his way, the dark copper blaze of her hair was the thing he had an eye for. The thought struck him: *Damn, they're twins!*

He had paid her this high tribute before quite realizing it, and at once he qualified the thought, admitting only that the sheen of the girl's hair exactly matched the chestnut's coloring. It was unfair to the chestnut to be called the twin of a nester girl, he was thinking, for he was inordinately proud of the animal. Still, the closer he got the more he had to admit that the comparison wasn't so bad after all.

He finally reined up the bank and in alongside the wagon's slewed-around front wheel and his lean face took on a grin he'd never thought he would be using on her kind. As he spoke, he touched the wide brim of his hat. "What's the matter, Chestnut? Trouble?"

Her green-mottled blue eyes flashed an immediate and bright defiance. "I've heard some peculiar questions," she said, her tone smooth and touched with a mocking softness, "but never one so insane as that. Yes, I'm in trouble. And my name's not Chestnut."

Bill liked them hot-tempered and now he was momentarily reminded of that percentage girl down in Socorro who had looked so kissable but hadn't been. She had turned out nothing but sharp nails and sharp tongue and, although she would have been trash alongside this girl, still they were alike in a certain way—the same way two unbroken, high-spirited colts are alike.

We'll string her along, he told himself, leisurely thumbing the wide hat onto the back of his blond head and letting his glance go to the half-buried rear wheel with a serious regard he didn't at all feel. The chestnut heaved a loud, relaxing breath to point up his slow inspection of the girl's predicament.

Bill shortly looked around at her again, then beyond to the posts marking the line of the ford. "Missed the shallows a bit, didn't you?"

"Another, exactly like the first," the girl breathed explosively, the line of her lips set tight in growing exasperation. She was obviously near the end of her patience.

"Another what, miss?"

"Another question."

"Like the first?" It took him a second or two to catch her meaning, and when he did, his smile came again, turning his face youthful and good-humored. "Yeah. Guess I'm just making words while I look the thing over. Have you tried hawing 'em around to line up the wheel so they can pull better?"

"I have."

"Didn't work, eh?" He scratched his forehead, eyeing the ox standing sleepily with head hanging. "Can't be much fun with one of them critters in harness."

"It isn't." The girl was looking across at him with a barely bridled anger. Her coloring and the delicate molding of her features were a rare combination and affected him queerly, giving him a strangely empty feeling. Then she was saying quite deliberately: "Now, if you've had your look and will be kind enough to move away, I'll try again."

He felt his face getting hot. "Beg pardon for the look, miss. But we don't often run into your kind, me and Red here." He had spoken without realizing exactly what he was saying. After all, wasn't she a nester?

His words brought a change in her glance, one of outright embarrassment. "I didn't mean me. It was the way you looked over the wagon. As though there was nothing to be done about it."

"Oh, that," he said. "Well, you'll admit you've got the thing hung up real good."

"I'll get it out."

"Looks like a busted axle back there."

Now her embarrassment faded before a deep concern. She leaned out so she could see back beyond the hickory-bowed tarp arched over the wagon's bed, studying the look of the big wheel down in the water. "Does it mean I can't go on?"

"We'll have to see."

Bill took his rope from the saddle and shook out a wide loop, and, watching him, she noticed that he did it without once looking at the rope or his sure, long-fingered hands. He kneed the chestnut out in front of her ill-assorted team and tossed his loop expertly over the tongue end. Now she couldn't take her eyes from him, marveling at his sureness and economy of motion. She saw him take two turns of the rope about his horn and touch the chestnut lightly with spur. The rope tightened and the tongue came on around squealing a complaint, the Grulla stepping nervously sideways and the ox coming along reluctantly.

Once the tongue was lined properly, Bill flicked his rope free and rode on back to put the chestnut into the stream. He had a boot and one leg underwater halfway to his knee as he leaned over and reached down into the swirling brown water, laying a tie onto the wheel hub. When the rope was tight, he came on up abreast the ox and took his turn around the horn again. Then he looked back at the girl and said: "Let's go. Give 'em hell."

Virginia Rush didn't like him, she told herself. Not a bit. A decent man didn't curse in a woman's presence. Nor did he mock her the way this stranger had with his smile when he had first come up. Another thing was that if a man insisted on wearing woolen underwear in this balmy weather, he should roll it up so his shirtsleeves would hide it instead of wearing it to his wrists with the shirt rolled to the elbows. Still another thing was that he wore a gun.

It was a big gun and not pretty. Rather than the plain cedar handle, she would have liked to see one of horn or pearl; she had yet to learn the Westerner's reticence over carrying a pearl-handled weapon. But the mere fact of his wearing a revolver was something she held against him. True, she had seen few men not carrying arms these past three days since leaving the train in Laramie. But it was still wrong. She could tell by the worn spot along the thigh of this tall man's waist overalls that the holster thong was as much a part of his dress as the curled-brim Stetson hat or the yellow silk handkerchief about his neck that had left an unsightly line of contrasting deep tan and white against his skin.

Yet she supposed she was being a bit unfair with him, disliking him when he was really trying to help. And just then he spoke to cut her thoughts short. "Ready any time you are."

She slapped the ox and the mare awkwardly with reins and struck them across their backs with the braided leather whip. The mare acted as she had before, lunging back and forth. The ox simply leaned into the harness and didn't seem to be trying very hard.

It was the ox and Bill's chestnut, with little help from the mare, that turned the trick. The big rear wheels finally bit into the bank, bumped up, and over it.

Virginia heard water splashing out the end gate and sloshing around in the bed. She gave a quick look in under the tarp, crying: "Oh, everything's getting soaked!"

Bill reined the chestnut quickly on back until he was close below her. He stepped out of the saddle to the wheel hub and swung up onto the seat so close to her their arms were pressed together. He took the reins without a word. And as he commenced sawing the team back, she was acutely aware of his bigness and strength and of the wide span of his shoulders. Strangely enough she didn't think to move away from him, though there was a lot of the seat left on her side.

He got the ox and the mare moving together somehow, gradually backing the wagon toward the bank. He hoisted a boot to the brake, which she hadn't had the strength to manipulate, and as the rear wheels were suddenly dropping down the bank once again, he stepped on the brake and locked the wheels just clear of the water.

Virginia held her breath as the wagon hung there, the end gate low now and the water pouring out around it with a sibilant splashing into the gravelly shallows.

She said: "Thank you. You've saved our things a wetting."

"Where's your man?" Bill asked abruptly.

She thought deliberately of her answer before giving it. "He left right after breakfast and rode on into Rifle. I'm meeting him there this afternoon."

"It'll be late," Bill drawled. He was unaccountably sore, mad clear through. He stood up and raised the whip and belted the ox unmercifully across the hindquarters. The wagon lurched clear of the bank. Bill dropped the reins and climbed down and went back to look over the damage. She would have a man!

The axle was broken all right, or rather badly split along nearly three feet of its length.

The girl was standing there, close behind him, when he came erect. She wanted to know: "Is it bad?"

He lifted his shoulders and let them settle slowly, thinking a moment before he said: "Nothing that can't be fixed. But it'll take time."

"How do I fix it?" she asked worriedly. All the spunk was gone out of her now and she even smiled helplessly as she spoke, as though to sooth the sting of the things she'd said a while ago.

"You don't fix it." He frowned. "Got any wire?"

She nodded, relieved. "Barbed wire. Pat brought several rolls along thinking the stores in Rifle might be running short."

"They probably are," was his dry comment as he walked around and untied the rope that held the tarp taut at the back.

He went silently to work, noticing one thing that didn't quite tie in with his first judgment of what she and her man might be. The wagon was the best of its kind, a Peter Schutler, sturdy and built of hickory for just this kind of rough going. Inside, boxes and trunks and bales, every heavy article, had been roped down tightly with an orderliness that somehow tied in with the girl's look of neatness and freshness. She was an uncommon nester, unlike the ones Bill had seen, and, as he got to work, he wondered about that.

Later, while he rode upstream looking for a cottonwood log, she followed his suggestion and unharnessed her team, staking them out on grass. By the time he was back again and had levered the wagon's rear end up so there was room to drop the axle off, she had a fire going and a Dutch oven in the coals, and he could catch the tantalizing odor of beef cooking. He hadn't realized it was so late, time to eat the noon meal.

She helped all she could, but it was mostly heavy work. When she could leave her fire, she would come across and watch him. And presently she began talking. He figured it was mostly because she felt ashamed of having been so brusque with him and he was sparse in his answers, wanting to show her he wasn't a man to take such talk from a woman. Anyway, it didn't matter. She had a man.

Once she asked: "Did you ever hear of Theodore Markus?"

He just nodded.

"Is he to be trusted?"

"I wouldn't know, ma'am." He had nearly called her "miss" again. "He's a land agent, which don't make him count for much on the face of it."

"Have you ever seen this?"

He looked up and regarded a sheet of paper she was holding out to him. He took it from her finally, curious, having heard about it many times but never before having seen it. And now he smiled as the ornate headline in heavy letters across the top of the sheet caught his eye: *GOLD FROM THE SOIL.*

Below that, in smaller print, ran Theodore Markus's tempting story:

Settlers! Pioneers! Speculators! Our Boys in Blue!

A vast section of fertile land along Squaw Creek in beautiful untouched Western Wyoming is now open to homestead. Situated near the thriving metropolis of Rifle, this land offers limitless opportunities for men and their families wanting to make their fortunes by raising crops on land never before turned by the plow. Think of it! In one year, or at the most in two, you can be the owner of a quarter-section farm the likes of which cannot be found in any other part of our country—nay, in all the world!

COME ONE, COME ALL!

For information write Theodore T. Markus, Esq. Real Estate, Rifle, Wyoming

Or just head for Rifle without writing.

Beat the others!

First Come, First Served!

Bill looked at the girl and handed back the sheet.

"Well?" she said.

"The way I got it, this Markus horned in on a cattleman. Hogged some of his range." Bill squatted down and went back to wrapping the barb-wire about the axle, wondering if he could make it tight enough to hold. He guessed he could.

"Pat wrote him," Virginia said seriously. "He's saving us a choice piece of land."

"Another thing," Bill drawled without looking up. "I hear it didn't make much difference to the rancher. Fella by the name of Cable it is, Bob Cable. This Squaw Creek is nothing but a narrow strip of grass running up through the hills into timber. Anyone that goes up there will have to grub out trees and stumps and probably rock."

"But he told Pat it was a fine piece of land. The one he's saving us."

"Sure. He's after his money. What did you have to pay him?"

97

"Only fifty dollars."

Bill chuckled. "*Only* fifty. Why, ma'am, this Ted Markus didn't have to lay out a blessed nickel for that land. It's government land, same as most of what you see all the way from here to Laramie. He's just set himself up a tinhorn business. You don't need his say-so to move onto Squaw Creek. He's a plain joker, ma'am."

"He can't be!" She bridled. "And don't keep on calling me ma'am!"

He looked up at her, puzzled. "You said you had a man."

"I have. Pat's my brother."

Suddenly everything was all right again. Everything was fine. Bill couldn't help grinning as he thought: *All this fuss for nothing.* Aloud he drawled: "Beg pardon. Thought you were hitched."

"Well, I'm not! And not likely to be."

Something about the way he kneeled there, looking up at her, made her glance suddenly waver and drop away. As she walked back to the fire, Bill could see that the back of her neck was getting red.

He began whistling.

II

It was almost 6:00 that evening when Bill reined the team down Rifle's crooked street. His saddle was in the wagon, the chestnut was tied on behind, and he was sorry the afternoon was ended. Virginia had turned out to be as nice as she looked, nicer if possible. Once back there an hour or so ago he had realized she was making him talk as he never had before. He'd never known there were so many words in him as he answered her countless questions. What was the desert like and was it true the Spanish girls down in Santa Fe were more beautiful than any others and what did he know about Cochise and the Army's campaigns against the Chiricahuas?

Her father had served out here somewhere during the War Between the States, fighting Indians mostly, and he had got her to tell him what she could remember of his story. It had pleased him to watch her as she talked and he'd been doing just that back there the time when the team had wandered off the road. The wagon had been fifty feet to one side of the road and jolting over a rock shelf before he noticed. He liked the way she had laughed over his being so flustered, the mischievous look that came to her eyes when she told him he'd better mind what he was doing.

Damn, now that the drive was over, he would have to be thinking up a reason for seeing her again tomorrow—and the next day, and the next, if he had anything to say about it. He hadn't stopped to think out why she was the only girl he'd ever wasted much of a thought over. But such was the fact and he was sort of proud of his realizing it.

This was a joke on him, he was thinking, his driving a nester wagon into a cattle town when he'd never before had a thing to do with a nester except maybe to chouse one away from some stream or water hole that belonged to whatever outfit he happened to be riding for.

That was a tricky point when you came to look at it. None of the cattle outfits really owned the grass they called theirs—or blessed little of it at best. It boiled down to a matter of how much a man could hang onto, how tough he could make it for anyone trying to move in on him. The big spreads stayed big because they could hire big crews and assert their power. Once in a while, like right here on Squaw Creek, a bunch of these homesteaders would try at filing on government land, considered open range by the cattlemen. Sometimes the homesteaders made it stick, but more often they were pushed on. And if they made a fuss, they were likely to be burned out, shot at, sometimes even killed. Bill wondered what the story would be this time.

Oddly enough, he didn't mind sitting this wagon and driving the lop-sided team for Virginia Rush. Virginia. He liked the name. It sounded right on a man's tongue. Gin or Jenny weren't too bad, either. Maybe when he really got to know her, he'd call her Virg, which was best of all.

His thoughts came back to the present at sight of a man sitting slackly astride a buckskin horse, heading up the street toward the wagon. It was the horse first of all that took his eye. The animal could almost be put alongside the chestnut and hold up its head—a little skimpy in the barrel, maybe, but a nice piece of horseflesh nevertheless. Then Bill noticed the way the man was riding the animal. And the bile rose in him.

A man can punish a horse without striking him and Bill saw at once that this man was punishing the buckskin. The way he sat, cocked to the side in the saddle, threw the animal off stride. And as he came on up to the wagon, he kept yanking at the reins, making the horse toss his head in a way that was pretty to see but that made no sense when Bill noticed the ornate spade bit.

He could almost feel the cruel jab of that bit against his own tongue as the stranger came abreast the wagon's team, calling out: "Howdy, folks! Welcome to Rifle. Now, if you'll keep right on down to the end of the street, I've got a nice campground laid out. Wood for your fire and water aplenty. Markus is the name, Theodore Markus. Glad you're here."

Theodore Markus had a too-hearty manner and an obvious flair for words. He was completely bogus for Bill's money. His gray eyes were set too close to the bridge of his hawkish nose and their cool gaze didn't back his outward affability. He was a narrowly built scarecrow of a man somewhere in his middle thirties and clad in somber black. His face had a sallow look, probably from too much bad whiskey.

But worst of all was that way he sat his saddle all out of kilter and mistreating the horse with the bit. With most horses that wouldn't have mattered to Bill, but to treat a good one this way got his dander up.

By now he had reined in and Markus had stopped. It was Virginia who answered the land agent, saying pleasantly: "I'm Virginia Rush. Has my brother seen you?"

"Certainly has, he certainly has, Virginia. Pat's already gone out to look things over. Said to tell you he'd be back after dark. Now you two come along and I'll show you where to put the wagon." He glanced at Bill, brusquely asking: "Who's this?"

"Bill Wells. He helped me fix the wagon today," Virginia said.

Bill noticed a decided coolness to her tone, understanding that she, too, had taken some slight offense at Markus having addressed her so familiarly.

Markus turned now, saying a in a lordly way— "Follow me."— and led the way down the rough street.

This was a hill town and the street needed some dirt hauled to smooth the exposed ledges of rock. The wagon began jolting, and Bill had to stand on the brake now and then to keep from running over his team.

This news about Pat's not being here wasn't so good. It had worried Bill all day long to think Virginia had a brother loco enough to let her in for a thing like driving an awkward team all this way by herself. Didn't the fool know that all kinds of riff-raff were in the country now, swarming to Rifle to feed on Markus's sugary offer? Once in a while there were even Indians busting off their reservations. A white woman alone in this country was an unheard-of thing. So far as Bill knew there wasn't a carbine or a shotgun, even a handgun, back there under the wagon's tarp. Except his own, of course, which he had taken off and rolled up and thrust into a comforter behind the seat, it having seemed the polite thing to do so long as he was sitting alongside Virginia.

So he didn't think much of Pat Rush, what little he knew of him, and what Markus had just told them didn't much improve his opinion. Virginia had told him that Pat had worked out here five years, "riding to cows", as she put it. Then along early in the spring she'd had this letter from him sending her railway fare, along with one of Markus's throw-aways, urging her to give up teaching in Alton and come out here to take up a homestead with him—two homesteads, in fact, for she was just of age and he wanted her to file on one along with his filing on one. Pat must have given her a tall story about what she'd find, because no girl in her right mind—especially one who'd never worked with her hands—would let herself in for this life if she knew the least bit about it. This was a man's country, still wild in a lot of ways, lusty and bawdy in a great many more, with short summers and killing winters. It was no place for a town-bred girl.

They were rolling down between the false-fronted stores and saloons now. A few lights were already on in the windows and the walks were crowded in front of the saloons. There were saddle horses and light rigs tied at the hitch rails and Bill idly noticed that every now and then Markus's head would bob or he'd lift a hand as he greeted someone along the awninged walks.

All of a sudden a high-pitched feminine voice screeched out over all the other sounds: "Hi yuh, hayseed! Who you got there, Markus? Tell him to pull the straw out of his ears! Hey, farm boy, leave that hoity-toity thing and come on in for a good time!"

Bill looked over and saw who had called, a woman leaning in a second floor window over a saloon, the Trail. He felt his face go hot and growled: "Someone ought to shut her mouth." But then he had to grin, for he saw that Virginia was doing her best to keep from laughing.

"I'm the one that's the hayseed, Bill," she said. "You can't be enjoying this much. These people know that I'm green."

He looked quickly around at her. "If I wasn't, d'you think I'd be here? Besides, there. . . ."

Bill never had a chance to finish. For just now, with the woman at the saloon calling out again, the wagon gave an abrupt lurch. The seat dropped from under Bill, and he came down hard on it again, and then Virginia was sliding down against him. He'd have fallen out, she on top of him, but for his grabbing a hold on the seat brace.

There they sat, the wagon tilted awkwardly down on its side, one wheel lying flat in the ruts.

He said—"Damn!"—and this time Virginia saw nothing out of the way in his language. She even had the feeling it might help to repeat his word.

Markus had stopped and was looking around, surprised, as Bill swung aground to regard the freshly broken rear axle. Bill was smiling and Virginia found she liked his look when it was this way as he glanced up at her and drawled: "Well, it got us here anyway. Now you can get it fixed proper."

The woman over the saloon was laughing bawdily now, cackling: "Get that junk off the street. You're blockin' the way, sodbuster!"

Markus came on back with a look of scowling impatience as Bill squatted down to survey the damage. The axle was broken clear through, Bill saw, and if it weren't for three or four windings of the barb-wire still holding it together, the whole thing would have gone over when the wheel came off.

A wrathful impotence held Bill as he sized up the situation. The wagon blocked the street. It had slewed around and there was barely room enough at either side for saddle horses to get past. Already a spring wagon was stopped close above, waiting to pass. People were gathering on both walks. There was a lot of laughing and jeering that Bill sensed was directed chiefly at Markus, not at these homesteaders he'd brought in. Usually in a spot like this the onlookers would have been only too willing to help. But not a man came out to offer any.

Now half a dozen cowpunchers, obviously together and probably from the same outfit, sauntered out from the front of the Trail between two tied ponies and stood close by, watching amusedly. One of these—a thick-set man with bowed legs and a chest full and deep as a nail keg—eyed the cocked-over wagon and team and Bill heard him say idly: "You can't file on that quarter-section, stranger. The town council would raise hell."

There were a few more laughs. Markus's angry voice sounded over them: "Horse, mind you no trouble now!"

Bill walked over and offered Virginia a hand. "Better get down," he said. "This thing may go on over."

Her face was red with embarrassment as she took his hand and stepped lightly down off the wheel hub. The man, Horse, took this moment to reach up and, with a grand gesture, doff his flat-brimmed hat and throw his arm across his waist, making a low bow, drawling: "Prince Charming and his lady. Light from your carriage, Princess."

The crowd loved it and a ripple of stronger laughter sounded from both walks. Bill's hard glance rocked around to Horse. But Horse was ignoring him now as he put his hat back on and, with a look of meaning, said to his men: "Boys, we could help make some room here."

Markus heard that and his indignant look changed to one of alarm. All he could think of was to repeat his warning of a moment ago, but this time in a pleading voice. "No trouble now, gents! Let 'em be!"

Horse winked broadly at the others. "Fred," he said, "lay

some iron on our friend Ted, here."

He had no sooner spoken than one of the others, a thick, slat-bodied individual, leisurely drew a long-barreled Navy Colt from his belt, cocked it, and lined it at the land agent. "Stay there, Ted," he said. And with that the other five, led by Horse, made for the wagon.

All at once Bill knew what they intended. His temper came wickedly on edge and his right hand dropped to thigh. But all he felt there was the empty expanse of his pants leg. His gun, of course, was in the wagon. A feeling of helplessness and bafflement flooded through him. He looked at Virginia. The blazing defiance she directed at the cowpunchers made him wince at what he knew was coming.

Then, and afterward, he knew that a woman had no place horning in on such a thing. A woman mixing in such a set-up robs it of its male dignity. Nevertheless, just now as Horse and his friends walked in toward her, Virginia said: "You touch this wagon and I'll have you all arrested!"

Horse stopped in his tracks, the others with him. The crowd went suddenly quiet with expectancy. Mock surprise came to Horse's blunt face. He said: "We're at your service, ma'am. Just trying to oblige you and him." His glance idly and scornfully touched Bill.

It was obvious that his politeness was a sham, that neither he nor the others—or the crowd, even—had any respect for these two supposed nesters Markus had brought in. That was eloquently demonstrated the next moment as a man behind Horse remarked tartly: "Let's get on with it." And he came on past Horse. Then they were all moving in again.

Virginia cried: "Bill, don't let them do it!"

Horse was almost abreast him when Bill made a last attempt at staving off what was happening. "Everything here belongs to the girl," he said. "This'll be rough on her."

But Horse only gave him a look of disgust, asking dryly: "Hiding behind your woman's skirts, fella?"

Bill gave way to an instant's reckless urge. He thrust out a boot and tripped Horse. As the man went off-balance, Bill lifted a long, looping uppercut, all the weight of his heavy shoulders behind his fist. His knuckles caught Horse along the shelf of the jaw and Horse went down loosely, never having caught himself since his boots tangled.

Bill barely had the time to swing around on the next man before a third was piling onto his back. He staggered, tried to double over and throw the man. But the weight was too much for him and he went on over and sprawled face down into the gravel. Another piled down onto him, and while they held him— one with knees at his shoulders, the other sitting on his legs— the two remaining men went on.

Bill heard the axle crack. There was a squealing of boards. Virginia was crying out something. Markus was shouting lustily and the crowd was letting out a roar of delight. Then the man on top of Bill beat his face down into the gravel and his senses went reeling dizzily away.

He was drowsily aware of the weight leaving his back and legs. He opened his eyes and lifted his head, tasting the salty tang of blood on his lips. Close beside him he heard Virginia sobbing, saying: "Won't someone even bring him a drink of water?"

Then after several more seconds rough hands rolled him onto his back and the shock of cold water splashing in his face brought Bill around, gagging for breath. He sat up awkwardly, wiping the water from his face, feeling a little pain in his nose and at his mouth.

He stared around in bewilderment. Virginia stood there, looking down at him with a pitying glance. A black-garbed man was alongside her, a nickel-plated star showing at the pocket of a gray vest under his coat. Beyond, showing indistinctly against the dusk, Bill could see people milling around the wagon. The wagon lay on its side now, the spokes of its cocked wheel etched against the darkening cobalt of the already star-studded sky.

"Better?" asked the man with Virginia.

"Yeah."

Bill got his knees under him and managed to stand. He was feeling mad again, and for a moment his eyes scanned the faces of the crowd, looking for Horse and the others. When he didn't see them, he said: "A hell of a thing, Sheriff, letting 'em kick a woman around this way."

The man's dour expression didn't break as he drawled: "I didn't let 'em do anything. I was down there at Markus's camp, sorting out some other trouble when this happened. You feel all right?"

It was embarrassing to have Virginia step up now and wipe the blood from his face with her handkerchief as he was answering: "Sure. Where's Markus? And this Horse and his crowd?"

"Gone, all of 'em. They had to carry Horse away. Fella, you could've done better than to get Crow Track riled at you. You're going to be living with 'em a long time up Squaw way if you settle here."

Virginia turned and said: "I've already told you this man isn't with me, Sheriff. He was only helping."

"So he was," the lawman said tiredly. "Well, this is just one more thing. There's five times as many people down there as can settle on Squaw Creek. So Markus is sicking 'em on Cable, on land that's rightly Crow Track's." He gave Bill a harassed look, his seamed and mustached face set doggedly. "I'm sure sorry there's no one to help you, stranger. But these people ain't in a mind to do much for Markus."

"We'll get along," Bill said.

He walked over to the wagon now and reached in to find the

comforter. There was a trunk lying on it and he had to lift the trunk before he could get at his gun. He jerked it out, his temper still at the boil, and, facing the loose circle of curious onlookers, he belted on the weapon. Then he eyed the crowd, asking: "Anyone got stomach enough to lend a hand here?"

First one man, then a second, stepped sheepishly in on the wagon. Bill said—"Thanks, the rest of you."—in a dry way that brought still another. Then someone said: "Come on, let's all pitch in." And before Bill realized it there were a dozen men at either end of the wagon lifting it upright again. Someone rolled an empty beer barrel across from the Trail and put it where the missing wheel should have been, and then a burly individual with a full spade beard was stepping up to Bill to ask: "You want me to do the iron work? My forge is still hot."

"Sure. And much obliged."

"If you'd get on down to Ramsey's real quick, he might let you have an axle."

"Who's Ramsey?"

"Hardware store. On down there past that big light."

The blacksmith walked down the street with Bill, and Ramsey let him have the axle, which Bill lugged back up to the wagon by himself. In no time at all the blacksmith was there, bolting on the new axle. The whole thing didn't take longer than half an hour, with so many hands helping, and when Bill finally paid off the blacksmith and helped Virginia back up onto the seat, the crowd gave them a ragged cheer.

They were farther on, near the single cross street, when Bill really looked at Virginia for the first time since he had picked himself up out of the street. "Not so bad after all, eh?"

"The fools!" she blazed. "I could have killed them." Abruptly her anger died out. "Thank you for what you did to that one man, Bill."

He chuckled softly. "Put him to sleep, did I?"

She nodded and her look became grave. "Your face, Bill. Doesn't it hurt?"

"No." He noticed they were approaching a building with a faded sign across its false front—*Range House*—and he asked: "Hadn't you better put up at the hotel?"

"Of course not," she said. "I'll want to be with Pat. We have a tent and I'm no better than the rest of these people. Where do you suppose the campground is?"

"We'll have a look."

They found the vacant lot Markus was using for his homesteaders down by the creek at the bottom of the street. Four or five supper fires were burning and Bill found room for the wagon along the back fence of the lot. Their arrival attracted several homesteader families who had doubtless heard of what had happened up the street and several men helped Bill unload the things Virginia needed, and then set the inside of the wagon to rights.

He was finished and throwing his saddle on the chestnut when Virginia noticed and came across from the fire. "You're not staying for supper?"

"Thought I'd mosey on up the street and eat a bit."

"You'll do no such thing," she insisted.

So he let the cinch hang loosely and tied the chestnut to the wagon again, then went on over to the creek to wash up. The water made the cuts on his face smart and for a minute or two he wondered if his nose was broken. But it seemed all right, solid enough, and now he could look back on the ruckus and get a little satisfaction out of remembering the solid feel of the punch he'd handed Horse. The man's jaw would be sore a sight longer than it would take the scratches on his own face to heal and it was good to be able to think that.

Virginia acted differently at their supper. She seemed shy and didn't often look straight at him, and now they both seemed to find a hard time scraping up anything to say.

It was Virginia who finally worded the thought that was troubling both of them. "Where are you headed from here, Bill?"

He shrugged. "No place in particular."

There was a momentary gladness in her eyes. "You might stay here, then?" she asked before seeing how transparent her words were. Then she added quietly: "No, I suppose there's nothing to keep you."

"Might ask around and see if any of the big layouts need an extra man," he said. "Trouble is, calvings over and they're laying off their crews instead of hiring. Maybe I'll just drift on to a fresh place."

She had nothing to say to that and he wondered at his own orneriness at having told her what he had. Then he gradually realized it was his wanting to be sure she'd like to see more of him that had made him speak the first thing that came to mind. Well, if her look of disappointment now meant what he thought it did, he had his answer. He was sure going to look around for a job here, he told himself.

When he couldn't think of another excuse for staying at her fire—when the dishes were done and put away and her tent pitched and his second smoke finished—he said: "Well, got to be moving. Sure you don't want me to hang around until Pat gets back?"

She smiled up at him. "No. I'm going to get some sleep, Bill." She sobered and added softly: "You were fine to help the way you did. Pat will want to thank you. Where will you be?"

"No telling."

She stood up now, offering him her hand. "Maybe we'll see more of you, Bill."

"Maybe."

She came over to the chestnut with him and he was tightening the cinch when she made more words, trying to take away the awkwardness of their parting. "If you're ever back through here again, stop up along Squaw Creek to see us."

He stepped into the saddle, his lean face slashed with its infectious grin. "By that time you'll have a man. He might not look kindly on a stray dropping in to see you."

"He would certainly make you welcome," she said with a surprising vehemence. "Besides, there won't be any man except Pat."

"Now you don't count on being an old maid, do you, Virginia?"

That was a fool thing to ask, he was thinking. And the answer he got threw the thing strictly in his lap as she said: "It's up to the right man, Bill."

He could have asked her if she'd run into the right man yet, but didn't, unaccountably flustered at the prospect of what she might say. So all he did was rein the gelding out, lift a hand, say—"See you later."—and ride back out to the street again.

The idea of sleeping in a hotel room didn't appeal to him. He put the chestnut in the livery barn, gave the hostler 50¢ extra, and crawled up into the loft. For a long time he lay there, thinking about the day, about Virginia.

His last waking thought was: *Now wouldn't it stack the deck if Crow Track would hire me on?*

III

Part of Bill Wells's philosophy was that doing the unexpected sometimes paid off. So the next morning, after a brief look downstreet at the smoke haze of the homesteader fires, he got breakfast at a restaurant, asked his way to Crow Track, and took a trail west from town into the lower foothills. He wasn't in a hurry and the twelve-mile ride took him almost two hours.

Riding in on Crow Track's headquarters, he was impressed

by the look of the layout that sat in a bay of the timber heading a mile-long meadow of lush grass. A clutter of buildings and corrals surrounded the main house, which was set against the backdrop of the pines and was L-shaped, built of logs.

Almost the first man he saw as he was riding abreast the biggest of the corrals was Horse. The man was afoot, walking between the barn and what Bill assumed was the bunkhouse. He saw Bill, stopped, and turned squarely to face him. And Bill, more amused than grudging over what he remembered of the fight on the street in Rifle, rode straight in on him.

Bill reined in half a dozen yards short of the man, folded his hands on the horn of the saddle, and, grinning down, said: "If you think I'm here looking for trouble, have another guess."

The look of stoniness that had been etched on Horse's face melted slightly. It took him a full five seconds to say: "I never make guesses. What's on your mind?"

"A job, friend. A job."

Horse gave a visible start. "You? Work here?" he asked. "For me? Hell, man, I rod this outfit!"

"Makes no difference," Bill said. "I'm looking for work. If you're so much of an old woman you can't forget a lucky punch someone landed on you in a ruckus you started yourself, then I had a wrong hunch riding all this way."

"Who says I'm an old woman?"

Horse instinctively reached up to the swelling alongside his jaw. It was then that Bill's infectious grin seemed to crack the shell of the man's reserve, for he said ruefully: "Brother, you'd remember if you'd been on the receiving end of that mule kick. Maybe it was luck, maybe not." He eyed Bill respectfully a moment before asking: "What can you do?"

"Rope, break, or shoe cayuses, mend fence, dig post holes, milk cows, drill a well, cut timber, de-horn a steer, butcher out a. . . ."

"Whoa!" Horse cut in, smiling now. "Unless you're a liar, I could fire the crew and sit back to watch you run the outfit yourself." His expression changed to a serious one. "Fact is, I let three men go last month. From now on all we do till fall is cut and pitch hay along with our regular chores."

"Maybe I didn't mention pitching hay. But you never saw a better man with a fork."

Horse frowned. "I don't get it. I thought you were a nester."

Bill shook his head. "Not so long as I'm sound of limb and head. That girl was in trouble yesterday. I helped her out. If I had the time to wait till you got an answer, you could write Andy Havers at the Double X over Bear Valley way. He'd tell you I'm a top hand. Also lazy and good for nothing."

Horse's look sharpened. "Havers sends a rep over here for roundup every year. You been working for him?"

Bill nodded.

"Why'd you quit?"

"Wanted to see some new country."

"This ain't far enough to be new country."

"Depends on how a man looks at it," Bill said. "It's far enough to suit me for a while."

Horse's glance was studying Bill closely as Bill took out a sack of tobacco and sifted some of the weed onto a wheat-straw paper. When he tossed the sack across, asking—"Well, how about it?"—the move startled Horse, catching him off guard.

For Horse's thinking was working along an odd channel now and he spoke before a certain idea was quite formed, saying: "We got more help than we rightly should have. Except for one thing."

"What's that?"

"Someone with a level head to deal with these grangers filing on that Squaw Creek stretch. I can't get along with 'em . . . neither can any of the rest of the boys."

"They're just plain folks, Horse."

"So they tell me." Anger toughened the look of Horse's blocky face. "But when one of 'em runs me off my own grass with a rifle, I don't quite know how to take it."

"That happened?"

Horse nodded. "Yesterday afternoon, clear the hell and gone up in the hills. A mile or so above the line the boss set as the highest these nesters could go. Young fella up there was piling rock to mark one corner of his quarter-section. I was real polite, telling him he was in the wrong spot. So he reaches behind this tree and the first thing I know I'm looking down the bore of a Thirty-Thirty. Mighty convincing, it was."

Bill thought a moment. "So that'd be my job, dealing with hotheads like that?"

Horse's head tilted in the affirmative. "That or nothing. The boss is dead set against starting any trouble. We think he's gone loco, treating these sodbusters so kindly. Burn a few ounces of powder now instead of a few pounds later, we say. But the old man sees it different."

"Then I'd have the job molly-coddling all hands and keeping everybody in a spirit of brotherly love?"

"That's about it," Horse said. "You'd have maybe the same chance as a tumbleweed in a dust devil. And you'd get fired so quick your head would sing if you made a wrong move. Lord, man, I been expecting to get my walking papers any day. If the boss hears about that shenanigan in town with you yesterday, I may be on my way out."

Bill weighed the man's pessimistic tone along with the prospects of the proffered job. They were anything but pleasant to contemplate, familiar as he was with the thousand and one prickly points working against any meeting of minds between cattlemen and homesteaders. Still, he was remembering Virginia right now and it didn't take him many seconds to say: "Horse, you just hired yourself a minister of state. What's the first chore you got for him?"

It took Horse even less time to give his answer. "Go up there along Squaw Creek, find that stray, if he's still there, and move him down where he belongs."

IV

Following Horse's directions, around noon Bill set out across the hills headed for Squaw Creek, forking a branded Crow Track steel-dust bronco and a week's supply of Crow Track grub in his bedroll. He would twice each day ride the line of a certain fence that marked the uppermost limit to where the homesteaders might file. Horse was leaving it entirely up to him on how to move out anyone who tried to move in above this fence.

"Handle 'em gentle," Horse had told him somewhat worriedly as they parted. "Otherwise, you lose your job and I lose mine." He added that Bill was to use one of the Crow Track's line shacks up Squaw Creek as his headquarters.

As it turned out, Bill never did see that line shack. For Horse had asked him first to ride past the spot where the rebellious nester had been putting up his location marker the afternoon before. Bill found the marker easily enough. And, close by, he found something else.

The man lay face down in a patch of pine seedlings not twenty feet from the monument he had erected. He might have been sleeping, Bill thought at first, until he noticed the way the blond head was cocked around, propped awkwardly off the ground by one bent-over seedling in a position that would have been unbearable to a live man. Then he saw the red smear patterning the torn back of the brown flannel shirt and he breathed involuntarily: "Horse, begin packing your possibles."

A small suspicion grew into a terrible certainty less than two minutes later, after he'd come aground and cleared away enough rock from the monument to uncover a tomato can buried underneath. The can contained a scrap of paper. On the paper, written in a crude hand, was a notice proclaiming this monument to be a corner marker of half a section of land comprising two homestead claims filed on respectively by Patrick and Virginia Rush. Sight of those names made Bill catch his breath. He exhaled a slow sigh and, tossing the can aside, walked over and took a deliberate look at Pat Rush. Although the face was blank-featured in death, the blue eyes open and staring, there still remained a certain carefree rashness of expression that told Bill he would have liked Pat, that hinted at a kindred spirit.

Turning away, Bill looked at his watch. "Two hours and thirty-four minutes," he said softly. "Shortest time you ever worked for any one outfit, fella."

He found Pat's horse, a gray, staked out on a patch of grass alongside the creek several rods to the east. A saddle and a bedroll hung from a lower branch of a thin-leaf cottonwood close by. Bill left the saddle where it was and used the bedroll tarp to wrap the body in. The gray was skittish and nervous about taking the load, but finally Bill had it roped on securely. When he left the spot, he was in his own saddle, leading the gray.

There was a gate through Crow Track's fence a mile below. Less than three hundred yards beyond that he came to the first homesteader camp. Two men, a woman, and a pair of kids eyed him suspiciously as he rode in on their crude lean-to, and, reining in just short of them, he announced unceremoniously: "Got a dead man here. Any of you know Pat Rush?"

"Rush?" echoed the older of the men. "Sure. He come by here yesterday at dinner time. Et with us." Suddenly his eyes widened. "That's him you got there?"

Bill nodded. His head was still moving when the second man made a dive for the lean-to and a rifle that stood slanted against its front post.

Bill lifted the .45 from his thigh in no special hurry. As it dropped into line, the man abruptly halted in his tracks and lifted his hands.

"Now let's keep off the prod," Bill said. "If I'd done Pat in, would I be here now?"

The homesteader gulped, his Adam's apple bobbing along his scrawny neck as he said stubbornly: "You would be if you was warnin' us off like Pat said one of your bunch tried to yesterday."

"Well, you can have another guess," Bill said mildly, holstering his weapon. "All I'm after's help. If one of you would take Pat on down to town, the other might come along and help me look things over up there. The sheriff ought to get up here fast as he can."

"Along with Markus," the other put in.

Bill nodded. "Suit yourself about Markus. But bring the law." He judged that the one who had been headed for the rifle had by now forgotten it, and with this assurance his eyes left the man and he swung aground.

When he looked back toward the lean-to again, it was to see the Winchester at the man's shoulder. The cold look of the eye staring over the sights warned him against moving even before the homesteader ordered: "Grab for some sky, stranger! There's nothin' I'd like better than to put you alongside Pat! Just try goin' for that hogleg!"

Bill's hands lifted slowly to the level of his shoulders. The older man came around behind him and jerked his Colt from his thigh.

As the hard snout of the .45 jabbed against his spine, the homesteader behind said: "Easy, Sam. We'll take him on in. Now I know how we're goin' to stretch that new rope we bought yesterday."

V

Rifle's jail was as solid as any Bill had ever seen, as dark and dank and cold as a root cellar. The only source of ventilation was the chimney of the rusted stove and a crack over the nail-studded oak door that must have been four inches thick. The room's only light also came through that crack between the door and its frame.

Bill had remarked dryly on this fact when the sheriff was locking him in, saying: "Keep me in here and I'll go blind. Like a mule in a mine. How about a lantern, Sheriff?"

"So you can burn your way out? Uhn-uh," had been the lawman's terse answer. "And you needn't worry about going blind. Takes a mine mule years for his eyes to go back on him. You won't live near that long."

"Then how about something to lie on?"

"You got nothing to rest up for except that climb up those thirteen steps."

With that acid rejoinder, Sheriff Holly had closed the door, bolted and locked it. And over the four hours that had passed since then the feeling that he was in a tomb had gradually come to Bill. Now and then he could catch faint sounds from the street that lay a little over a hundred yards below, beyond the alley that led up this hill. At first he had built one cigarette after another. Then finally his throat became parched and he realized he must do something else to work off his nervous energy.

So he had tried to think his way out of there. But he had to discard idea after idea until finally no other would come. Riding up from the street with his hands manacled to the horn of his saddle, he had noticed carefully that the jail was built of rock slabs, roofed with at least three feet of solid earth over its log joists, and the back third of its depth was dug deep into the face of a steep hill. One day he was to learn that the building had many years ago been a fort erected by the beaver trader who had been the town's first citizen, but just now he knew only that it seemed as indestructible as a granite boulder.

He had asked to see Virginia. The sheriff had turned him down flatly. "Hound that girl when she's already half crazy with heartache? Son, you've got snow melt in your veins."

But he couldn't keep Virginia out of his thoughts any more than he could help wondering at the way Pat had died. Now that it was all over he was regretting a few things. First, if he had it to do over again, he would spend a lot of time looking around up there near Pat's monument, looking for sign, anything that would point to who the killer could have been. And next, instead of bringing Pat's body on down as he had, he'd have ridden straight to Crow Track and had it out with Horse. Try as he would not to suspect Horse, he couldn't help but wonder just how much of the story Horse had given him was true, how much false. Had Horse sized him up as a fool and sent him to the end fence to take the blame for a killing that Horse had done himself? Or had Horse hired him on good faith, ignorant of what had happened to Pat?

What he wanted most was the chance of talking to Virginia, of hearing her say that she didn't believe what others must be believing, that he was Pat's killer. Thinking of her as she had been yesterday was the thing that steadied him, made him figure he had an even chance of talking his way out of this as soon as tempers cooled enough to let men listen to reason.

The light shining through the crack in the door was fading when he began hearing sounds he couldn't understand at first. There were many voices, some of them high-pitched, one of them vaguely familiar, echoing up from the direction of the street, and as he listened, he finally realized that there must be a crowd down there. Then abruptly he recognized that one familiar voice as belonging to Theodore Markus and a vague apprehension ran through him when the others died away and only Markus's voice continued on at a strident high pitch.

It was while Markus was still shouting outside that the padlock rattled against the door. Shortly Bill heard the bolt pulled back, and then the heavy door was swinging slowly open, its rusty hinges squealing.

Two figures stood outlined against the gloom of dusk beyond the opening. One was the sheriff and the other Bill was startled to see was Horse. The lawman stood with a drawn Colt in hand, and when the door stood wide, he planted a hand in the middle of Horse's back and pushed him roughly toward Bill, at the same time saying ominously: "You two can eat when things have calmed down. If they ever do."

Making sure that Horse was well out of reach, he reached in and started pulling the door shut.

Sight of Horse had roused a quick anger in Bill. Yet now he put that emotion aside to say quickly: "Sheriff, I've got to have a talk with Virginia Rush."

Sheriff Holly's low laugh was mocking. "You tell him what his chances are, Horse," he drawled mysteriously. And with that the door slammed shut.

The bolt was grating into place as Bill said tonelessly: "What did he mean?"

"That she won't see you, I reckon. They say she's going along with Ted Markus."

Bill was completely mystified and his anger toward Horse was gone as he asked: "Going along with him how?"

"Trying to talk that crowd into throwing a necktie party for us."

"For *us*?" Bill was dumbfounded on two counts. "You, too?"

"No one else." Horse's voice sounded rueful in the room's blackness. Bill heard him sigh gently before he added: "And, brother, we don't have too much time. That Markus could persuade a tribe of wooden Indians." As though to back his words, they could hear Ted Markus's voice rise to a higher pitch outside now.

"You could let me in on it, whatever it is," Bill said.

"Not much to let you in on," Horse said. "The sheriff came across for a talk with me about four, after he'd been up there on Squaw looking around. The minute I owned up to forkin' the nag that made that second set of tracks near where they found Rush, Holly unlimbered his hardware and I was under arrest. When I told him I'd run onto Rush yesterday afternoon, he told me to guess again. He claims either me or you went back there last night, riding the same jughead I forked during the afternoon, and drygulched Rush. Claims I had you run onto Rush this morning and bring the body down just to cover what we'd done."

Bill was having to make a lot of guesses to take all this in, for Horse hadn't by any means told him everything. Yet now, regardless of the seriousness of the things Horse was saying, he was remembering Sheriff Holly's parting words.

"But the Rush girl can't believe all this," he said incredulously.

"If she doesn't, she's got a poor way of showing it," Horse said. "The boss came on in with me. He's weak-kneed as usual. Went to see the girl. According to him, she just stood there with her face blank as a clean sheet of paper. When he'd quit talking, all she said was to tell you she was going to even the score for her brother. Said she'd known all along he hated you."

"All along?" Bill echoed incredulously. "Hated me? How could he when he'd never laid eyes on me?"

"He hadn't?" Horse asked. Then he added uncertainly, stubbornly: "Well, still that's what she said. The old man took particular pains to warn me against you."

Horse's brittle laugh told Bill how little stock he was putting in the rancher's belief and Bill was thankful for this slender encouragement as the shock of Virginia's words hit him. His disbelief changed gradually to uncertainty. And then quite sud-denly a notion hit him that made him say: "Horse, she's trying to tell me something."

"Sure she is. It's pretty plain. She'd like to see you hang."

"You're wrong," Bill said quickly, excitedly. "Don't you get it? I've never before seen her brother. She wants. . . ."

His words broke off momentarily as a shout echoed up from the street. And Horse said tartly: "This has played straight to that land-hungry son-of-a-bitch's hand. This afternoon he had the Rush girl file on that land her brother had picked. And he filed on the quarter-section above it himself. The boss is so upset over what happened, he's agreed to open up that extra mile of Squaw, give up some of the best of his grass. Now Markus is down there usin' the platform behind the Trail like a barker in a tent show. He's got a big crowd listening while he preaches justice against the land hogs, meaning any cow outfit in general and Crow Track in particular. If he can prod 'em into stringing us up, it'll mean more money in his pocket than he could hope to make in ten years the honest way."

"But this other," Bill said impatiently. "What Virginia said. She's going to even the score for her brother. And she knew all along Pat had hated me. Don't you get it, Horse? She must be onto something. She said that about Pat hating me just to let me know things look different than they really are."

"What things?"

"This play she's making against me. It doesn't hold water. She wouldn't have a reason to hate me."

"I don't get it, Wells."

"I don't, either. Not quite," Bill had to admit. "But you wait."

"For what?"

Bill sighed, saying softly: "I wish I knew."

As the next hour dragged past, he really did wish he knew what lay behind Virginia's mysterious words and actions. For a time he was uncertain of his hunch. Then finally his common sense told him that a girl like Virginia wouldn't turn against him without good reason. And the circumstances surrounding Pat's death weren't reason enough to have caused that. No, something else lay behind her strange behavior.

Once Horse went to the door and tried to see out through the slit along its top. But after several seconds he turned away, saying: "Too high. All I can see is the flickering of those torches down there. Markus had the alley lined with 'em." They could catch the voices of the crowd now and then, and one that spoke over the others, gradually silencing them, that Horse identified as Sheriff Holly's. "He's a good man," Horse said. "He'll be trying to talk sense into 'em."

But immediately after the lawman's voice went silent, Markus was speaking again and gradually, yet so surely that they could almost picture him tongue-lashing the onlookers, the pitch of his tones rose to a higher note. And other voices occasionally interrupted him with angry shouts.

Encouraged as he had been over the meaning he had put to Virginia's words with Cable, Horse's boss, Bill's hopes now gradually died to leave him bleakly aware of the possibilities the night might bring. Years ago he had seen a mob half kill an innocent man suspected of rustling. This mob—and it would surely become one in the end, if Markus kept on with his silver-tongued oratory—had far more provocation than the other and far less to lose in dealing with a man they saw as a killer.

"Horse," Bill said finally, when the shouting below had become almost continuous, "I'd a hell of a lot rather be in this alone than with you."

"Nothing's going to happen," Horse grunted. But his tone lacked conviction.

It was Bill who caught the soft rattle of the padlock some minutes later. The next second his whisper cut the darkness like a keen knife: "Get to the other side of the door, Horse."

He heard the scrape of Horse's boots as he moved in on the door, and then Horse said softly: "Damned if I don't butt a few heads before they put the hemp around my neck."

The stillness of the next several seconds was awesome and tense to Bill as he stood, flattened to the wall there alongside the door. He gave a start as he heard the bolt thud softly. Then the door hinges were squealing and he saw a narrow wedge of starlight replace the blackness of the door's rectangle.

One instant he stood crouched forward, knees bent, hands clawed, ready to spring. The next all the tension drained out of him and he was breathing, relieved, glad—"Virg."—seeing her slender shape silhouetted against the flickering light of the flares glowing in the alley below.

She must have liked his calling her that, for as he stepped into the doorway, she cried softly: "Oh, Bill." Then, before he quite knew it, she was in his arms with her head against his chest and his face was pressed into the soft mass of her chestnut hair.

He could catch its fragrance and feel her trembling against him, and it was perfectly natural that he should stroke her head gently with one hand, saying: "We knew you weren't forgetting us, Virg."

She drew away a little now, her head tilted back as she looked up at him. He was surprised to see the glistening of tears in her eyes as she said in a choked voice: "Bill, everything's gone wrong. If I'd only known."

"Everything's fine," Bill told her.

He caught her look of astonishment. "When they're down there talking about hanging you?" Her voice was hushed. "When Markus has forgotten what he promised me?"

"And what did he promise?" Bill asked as he heard Horse move in behind him.

"He was with me when they brought the news of Pat," Virginia said in a tone she had a hard time keeping steady. "He believed me when I insisted you were innocent. But he said, if I pretended to believe you were guilty, that maybe the man who did it would . . . would overplay his hand. That's how he put it. He was sure someone from Crow Track had done it. He said that now was the time to teach all the cattlemen a lesson, to settle all the troubles the homesteaders have been having. It seemed I'd be doing something worthwhile, something Pat would have wanted me to do. So. . . ."

When she hesitated, Bill said gently: "So you went along with him?"

She nodded mutely and stood a moment looking up at him, her eyes pleading for his understanding. "Oh, I've said so many terrible things about you, Bill, thinking I was helping these poor people. I even thought Markus was right in paying those four men to take out land adjoining his and mine. He said it was one way of hitting back at Crow Track."

"So he's paid someone to help him grab a section or two of choice graze, has he?" Bill asked tonelessly.

"I don't know what he's done, Bill," she answered in a panicked, desperate voice. "Only I do know that it hasn't turned out as I thought it would. Instead of protecting you, as he promised, he's let those people get out of hand. He's down there preaching justice and fair treatment for the homesteaders. He must know that what he says is only strengthening the feeling against you, yet he's doing nothing to stop it. I stood it as long as I could, then I made up my mind to see him. I was going to threaten to tell those people how I really felt about you if he didn't urge them to be peaceable. I was working my way through the crowd when the sheriff took me aside and gave me the key."

"Gave you the jail key?" Horse, close behind Bill, asked

incredulously.

Virginia nodded. "Sheriff Holly was afraid they'd take it from him. So he asked me to keep it for him until the trouble blew over." She was looking pleadingly at Bill now. "I've broken his trust in coming here, Bill. But I was terribly afraid of what would happen if I didn't."

Bill said: "The luck's all ours. After we're gone, lock the door again and throw the key away. Tell the sheriff you lost it. Then, when they find we've gone, they'll think someone took it from you without your knowing."

"Will you write and let me know you're safe, Bill?" the girl asked. "I'm leaving here, going back to Laramie. I can wait there for a letter."

"I'll come myself instead of a letter."

"You mustn't!" she said quickly. "They'll be hunting you, even in Laramie. You must leave this country."

Bill was staring thoughtfully down at her. "Maybe he's overplayed his hand."

"Who?" came Horse's blunt question.

When Bill didn't answer at once, Virginia asked: "You know something, Bill?"

"Not for sure." He was trying to think something out, but his suspicion was too indefinite to risk sharing with anyone and shortly he said: "You're to wait here, not in Laramie, Virg. When you get back down there, pretend to go along with the others. When they find we've lit out, stick as close as you can to Markus. Watch what he does. Don't let him know you think he'd done wrong."

"How can I, Bill, when I don't even like him? And what good will it do?"

"Just this much," he told her. "He'll be in the thick of it. Sooner or later you'll hear from me and I'll want to know what's been going on." He reached out and laid a hand on her arm.

"Don't worry. Some night soon I'll show up there at your wagon down at the end of the street."

He turned from her now and touched Horse. "Let's be moving." Then as Horse came on past him, he pulled the door shut, shot the bolt, and snapped the padlock. The key was still in the padlock and he took it and threw it as far as he could off to the left, up the hill slope.

"Give us a two-minute start and then walk a big circle getting back down there," he told Virginia as he turned away from her, following Horse into the shadows.

As they were walking away, Virginia called softly: "Be careful, Bill. If anything should happen, I'd. . . ."

He wondered what it was she had started to say.

VI

They found the homesteader lot at the bottom of the street dark and deserted, the supper fires burned out. They didn't even have to be quiet in cutting a pair of horses from the bunch in the rope corral at the back of the lot and in helping themselves to a pair of saddles from one wagon.

Horse was all for taking to the hills, but Bill insisted on openly riding straight out the west trail toward Crow Track. "We'll make better time," he said.

Yet once they had started, Bill seemed to be lagging behind. And after the first mile Horse pulled up and waited long enough for Bill to come even with him, tartly asking: "What's the matter, your nag no good?"

"Sure she's good."

"Then why hang back?"

It was a long moment before Bill replied. And then he didn't answer the question but asked one of his own. "What you said about the sheriff thinking you'd gone back last night after Pat Rush, Horse. He found sign to prove it?"

"Sign to prove someone had gone in there. But not me, brother!"

"Y'know," Bill mused, "I'd like a look at that sign."

His words brought Horse's head swinging sharply around. And even in the faint starlight the Crow Track ramrod's expression showed strong amazement. "You'd what?"

"Like to go up there and look over that sign. Might tell us something."

"Uhn-uh," Horse was quick to say. "Not me. I'm headed over the pass just slow enough to keep from killing this jughead."

"OK, then you better get a move on," Bill said. "I'll just mosey along up Squaw Creek and have my look."

"And have 'em corral you sometime tomorrow? If," Horse added, "they don't do it sometime tonight?"

"By that time it won't matter much," Bill said. "By that time I'll have found what I'm after."

"Which is what?"

"Can't tell you yet for sure."

They fell silent, riding on at the leisurely trot Bill had been holding ever since leaving the town behind. Horse made no move to pull on ahead now. Bill sensed an indefinable air of tension building between them, and what he could make out of Horse's expression in the poor light showed him the man's face set dourly in anger.

Quite suddenly Horse burst out: "All right, I'll play the fool with you! But we don't have to take all night to do it!"

Bill chuckled softly and lifted his animal to a faster trot. From then on neither of them spoke. But when they came to the forks that angled north toward Squaw Creek, Horse swung into it ahead of Bill.

They were three-quarters of an hour riding the several miles up the Squaw Creek trail to the gate in Crow Track's fence, and another ten minutes beyond that to the monument Pat Rush had built yesterday to mark the corner of his half-section. All this way Horse had set the pace and now he reined in close to the marker's dark pyramid shape and waited for Bill, saying as he came alongside: "If you don't waste too much time, we can still make it over the pass before sunup."

"Yeah," Bill said absently as he swung aground. He looked first to the left, then toward the creek, shortly asking: "Now where's this sign?"

"Mine or the other ranny's?" came Horse's impatient query.

"Both. Yours first."

Horse swung his animal over twenty feet or so beyond the pile of rock. "Here's about where mine would be. Rush didn't even give me the chance to get down out of my hull."

Bill walked on over, dropping the reins to ground-halter his horse. And when he was close to the Crow Track man, he reached into a pocket of his shirt, took out a match, and thumbed it alight, stooping over to study the ground.

Horse said quickly, harshly: "Kill that light! You want 'em to spot us?"

"How'm I going to see without it?"

"See what?"

"Can't tell yet."

Horse grunted in impatience, said worriedly—"Then get on with it."—and watched as Bill held the match close to the ground and, bent over, walked a deliberate circle.

Abruptly Bill stopped and went to his knees. His match guttered out and he lit another. And presently he asked: "A flared shoe? The right front toed in some."

"That'll be the one," Horse said. "That mare got a bad kick from a stallion a year or so back. Thought she was crippled for good. But she came around fine."

"Now where did the law find the other sign . . . the tracks you made when you came back last night to get Rush?" Bill was grinning as he said this last.

"I shot him from behind that bunch of trees down there, according to Holly," was Horse's dry answer. And he nodded toward a clump of pines near the creek.

Bill walked down there, Horse following, sitting slackly in the saddle. When they reached the trees, Bill asked: "About here?"

"No. Behind 'em."

Bill walked around to the far side of the pines and there repeated what he had done out by the monument, lighting a match, walking slowly about, looking at the ground.

Suddenly there came a sound, distant and muted, that made Bill straighten and stand quite still. Horse turned in the saddle and stiffened. The sound came once more, deep-noted, eerie. Then Horse breathed: "God Almighty! That'll be Overholt's pack of lion hounds. Brother, let's make tracks!"

But Bill, after hearing the baying of the hounds riding the distance once more, said: "You go, Horse. I'm staying." And he had no more than spoken before he lit another match.

Horse drew in a quick breath, about to say something. Then he caught himself and the way he eyed Bill was strange, with a blend of helpless anger and respect. He saw Bill studying the ground again, saw him go to his knees as he had above near the spot where Pat Rush's body had been found.

Then Bill was saying: "Here it is. Same animal."

"Look, Bill," Horse said with a barely controlled impatience, "I've seen those dogs of Overholt's tear a bear to pieces so small there wasn't a hunk of fur left big enough to cover a man's hand. If we ride the creek a ways, then cut for the high country, we can still get away."

"From what?"

"Getting our necks stretched, damn it!"

Bill took time to light another match before he said: "There's no chance of that now, Horse. I know who did it."

"What?" Horse asked in an awed voice. "You know who killed Rush?"

Bill nodded, nothing more.

And after a few seconds Horse burst out: "Come on, tell me!"

Bill shook his head. "No, I don't think I will. Proving it's going to be something else again. And I'd rather you couldn't give it away."

Horse was about to protest that when the howling of the hounds sounded again, much closer now. Very faintly across the stillness echoed the hoof drum of running horses and that sound put a look of alarm on Horse's face. He said soberly: "Bill, you better either get onto your nag again or climb a tree. In about three minutes this place'll be swarming with the closest thing you ever saw to a pack of wolves!"

Bill nodded, flicked the match aside, and walked away. When he was back again, astride his horse, the Crow Track man said feelingly: "Hope you know what you're doing."

"I do. But it'd help if we had some light." Bill had no sooner spoken than he was swinging aground once more.

Horse knew better than to ask what he was doing and simply sat there until all at once Bill lit another match. When the light flared abruptly, Horse saw that Bill had touched off several handfuls of pine needles. Next, Bill collected several branches and, breaking them into small pieces, tossed them onto the small blaze.

The dogs were baying fiercely now, their howls lifting to a high yapping note as they scented their quarry. Reluctantly almost, Bill took that warning and climbed astride his horse once more. And less than ten seconds later the first pair of hounds burst through a nearby alder thicket and raced down into the light of the fire.

Both Bill and Horse had their hands full for the next minute as the other dogs came on in, tonguing excitedly as they joined the first pair in snapping at the horses' heels. Both animals pitched and tossed and reared, and Horse's tried to bolt but was hauled back close to the blaze that now burned more brightly.

Abruptly a rider appeared around the edge of the alders. It was Theodore Markus astride his leggy buckskin and he rode with a Colt in hand, leveling it at Bill and Horse, shouting: "Reach, you two!"

They tried to obey but were too busy managing their mounts to be able to let go the reins. And presently Markus turned and bawled loudly: "Over here! I got 'em!" At the same time he kept his distance.

Three more riders appeared as suddenly as Markus had, one of them coming aground and calling the dogs, cursing them into obedience until finally their clamor quieted and Bill and Horse could control their animals.

Markus said again: "Lift your hands!"

"Why?" Horse wanted to know. "We aren't packing irons." And he looked at the others.

Markus's narrow face contorted in rage. He was close to Horse and all at once reined his buckskin in on the Crow Track man. He struck so quickly that Bill's warning cry of—"Watch it, Horse!"—came a split second too late. By that time the barrel of the Colt had whipped down at the side of Horse's head. And Horse, after a brief grimace of pain, sagged sideways in the saddle and fell to the ground.

Another mounted figure rode into the light a moment later. It was Sheriff Holly. He said: "Was that called for, Ted?" With a glance of distaste at Markus he came down off his horse and walked over to the unconscious Crow Track ramrod.

He was kneeling there alongside Horse when the rattle of a light rig's tires against gravel sounded across the momentary stillness. Then Bill saw a team of horses moving in on the others. They were pulling a buckboard, and, as it came into the stronger light, he saw two figures sitting on the seat. One was the homesteader who had taken him in to the sheriff this morning. The other was Virginia.

Markus also noticed their arrival and, as the team came to a halt, he called: "Sam, turn around and take her back to your place! A woman's got no place here."

It was Virginia who answered: "I'm staying. You're doing nothing to these men until they have a chance to explain." And to back her words she stepped down to the wheel hub, and then aground. She walked over into the stronger light until she stood alongside Sheriff Holly, giving Markus a defiant stare.

For a moment he seemed uncertain. Then his glance shuttled to Bill. "You, Wells," he said crisply. "Get down."

Bill swung deliberately from his saddle and one of the dogs started for him only to be stopped by a shout from the man who had been busy tying them to a rope leash.

"Now," Markus said, "first you'll tell us who busted you out of that jail."

Bill ignored Markus, turning to Holly and Virginia. "Sheriff," he said, "we came up here hoping to find something to give us a line on who killed Pat Rush. This afternoon you told Horse that someone had come back here last night and shot Pat. Since. . . ."

"Why do we have to listen to him?" Markus interrupted hotly. He reached to the coil of rope tied below the horn of his saddle now in a gesture of unmistakable meaning.

Then one of the others spoke, saying mildly: "Hell, Ted, let him talk if he wants to. He can't get away."

"Sure, let him," another said. "Even a guilty man's got the right to have his say."

And as their attention centered on Bill again, Sheriff Holly asked: "What are you trying to tell us, Wells?"

"This man that got Pat last night," Bill said, "rode right in here behind these trees, according to what you told Horse this afternoon."

The lawman nodded. "That's the way it looked to me."

"And he forked the same animal Horse had during the afternoon, didn't he?"

Once again Holly nodded.

Bill turned away and took several steps back toward the pines. There he went down on one knee, pointing. "Here's his tracks. Take a look at 'em, Sheriff."

Frowning in puzzlement, Holly came on across. The fire's flickering light reached far enough so that he could see the hoof prints as Bill said: "Take a good look."

Holly studied the markings on the ground a long moment, saying finally: "Yes, those are the ones."

Bill looked back over his shoulder. "You, too, Markus."

Theodore Markus hesitated before finally coming down out of his saddle and walking across to join Bill and the sheriff. He still carried the gun in his hand and made it a point to keep out of Bill's reach. After a quick look at the ground, he said grudgingly: "All right, I see."

"Notice anything queer?" Bill asked, looking up at him.

"No." Markus was eyeing him with suspicion, warily.

"How about you, Sheriff? Notice anything queer?"

"Well . . . ," Holly hesitated briefly, then went on, "the fact is this afternoon I noticed that some of the prints are clearer than the others. And farther back they don't make a straight line."

Bill smiled thinly, nodding. "But why?"

The lawman shrugged. "I don't know."

Without their noticing it, Virginia had come over and was standing near Bill now. "Why, Bill?" she asked.

He came erect, saying: "Come along and I'll show you." And

he led the way over toward Horse and Markus's buckskin.

"Watch him, all of you!" Markus called out. "There's some trick to this."

Bill stopped at the fire long enough to pick up a branch blazing at one end. Then he kept straight on until he had walked in behind the buckskin. There he held the branch low to the ground, looking back over his shoulder at the sheriff as he said: "See if this means anything."

Holly and Virginia, with Markus closely following them, came up to him. The lawman looked deliberately at the ground, at length saying: "Nothing I can see. They're tracks, sure. But different ones. Made by Ted's horse there."

Bill nodded readily enough. "So they are. But let's follow 'em back a ways." And he led the way around the alder thicket along the line of the buckskin's tracks, holding the blazing end of the branch low to the ground. Now the rest of the sheriff's posse was coming along, following slowly.

After several more steps, Bill stopped abruptly. He glanced around at the sheriff, asking enigmatically: "See what I mean?"

Markus was quick to leave the lawman's side and step around Bill to inspect the ground, asking: "What?"

Bill pointed to the ground. "There, where your horse missed his stride."

"What're you trying to prove?" Markus asked irritably. "Does it mean anything if my horse missed his stride?"

Bill soberly tilted his head. "I'm afraid it does," he said quietly. "No horse but yours, walking straight and free across open ground, would step out to the side like this."

Markus was scowling at him, obviously trying to see what lay behind his words. "What's wrong with my horse?" he asked. "Who says his gait isn't steady?"

"Maybe I put it the wrong way, Markus," Bill said. "Maybe I should've said that any horse you ride is thrown off stride."

He glanced briefly at the sheriff now to see a look of wonder gathering on the lawman's face. Then Holly was saying softly, feelingly: "They're the same."

Bill faced Theodore Markus squarely now. "It was you, Markus. You must've been up here to see Pat Rush after he gave Horse his marching orders yesterday. That probably surprised you, to think that Crow Track had backed down from kicking a homesteader off their grass. It gave you an idea. Today you started working at your idea by filing on the quarter-section alongside this, by having Virginia file on her piece."

When he paused, Markus's glance shot helplessly toward the sheriff and on to the others. Then the man seemed to find his nerve again, for he laughed mirthlessly. "You're not talking sense, Wells. Of course I filed on this land. The law says I can. And Crow Track's damned well going to like it."

"That's what I've been saying," Bill agreed, too readily to suit Markus. "But do these other people know that you paid two or three saddle bums to file on land adjoining yours? That you aim to have their grass to throw in with yours? That maybe you'll buy Virginia's quarter-section, too? Do they know that last night you rode out to Crow Track, stole Horse's mare, and rode her in here and shot Pat Rush?"

Markus was smiling crookedly now in a brazen attempt to appear unconcerned. Yet his paleness betrayed him, that and the tremor in his tone as he said: "Go on, make a good story of it, Wells."

"Guess I will at that," Bill said. "Only I'll leave it to Pat's sister and the sheriff." He glanced at Virginia. "Virg, would you swear out a warrant on the man who killed Pat?"

"You know I would, Bill. Gladly." There was a strong expectancy showing in her now as she answered him.

"And you, Sheriff," Bill went on, his look shifting to the lawman. "Did you ever notice the way Markus sits his hull? All loose and off kilter, not giving the horse a chance?"

Holly nodded.

Bill's eyes swung quickly back to Markus. "You're done for, neighbor," he said. "Virg's swearing out a warrant on you. Holly's had his look at those tracks and he'll testify against you. And there won't be a man on the jury that doesn't know enough about horses to figure the same as Holly and I do. Which is that you rode that Crow Track mare in here last night and bushwhacked Pat Rush."

Markus suddenly took a backward step, arcing up the Colt and lining it at Bill, his thumb crooked over the hammer.

He was about to say something when Bill said: "It's a shame you busted that hammer when you hit Horse."

Theodore Markus's glance dropped involuntarily to his weapon. A split second later Bill lunged in on him. Then Markus saw his mistake and tried to dodge aside. His thumb drew back the hammer of the .45 and he was swinging it frantically into line as Bill's lifting blow caught him along the jaw.

The Colt exploded deafeningly, its rosy stab of powder flame lining over Bill's shoulder. Then, as Markus sagged at the knees, Bill hit him again, and he went down loosely, unconscious even before he folded to the ground and rolled onto his side.

Bill stepped in and kicked the Colt from his hand. Then he heard a soft cry and turned to find Virginia there beside him.

As he took her in his arms, he looked beyond to the sheriff. "Now how do you reckon he figured he really could have busted that hammer?"

★ ★ ★ ★ ★

GUN PURGE AT TENTROCK

★ ★ ★ ★ ★

The author's title for this story was "A Gun-Purge Rides the Tentrock". It was submitted to John Burr, the new editor at Street & Smith's *Western Story Magazine* on June 12, 1939. It was purchased on July 17, 1939. The author was paid $67.50 at his word rate of 1 1/2¢. Peter Dawson's word rate at Street & Smith would continue to increase over the next decade. Upon publication in the issue dated October 28, 1939 the title of this story was changed to what it is now in its first publication in book form.

I

Sid Remington, Tentrock's foreman, walked his black gelding down the steep incline of the alley to halt finally within the impenetrable shadow of a lean-to in the rear of Hillton's Mile High Saloon. He sat a moment, warily studying the obscure darkness around him, then softly said: "Turk, that you?"

A shadow a shade lighter than that of the saloon's rear log wall moved across the narrow alley and took on a man's shape, and a voice said irritably: "Took you long enough to get here. A hell of a time to drag me in on a twelve-mile ride."

The Tentrock man swung from his saddle and ground-haltered the black, drawling: "Don't crow yet, Turk. You'll be glad enough you came."

Remington's high frame was accentuated by a gauntness that made his motions awkward and ungainly. His face was so thin that its bone-pattern bore a skull-like prominence, deep-socketed, cold gray eyes that were as clear an indication of his character as the twin belts and holsters he wore tonight along his thighs.

He asked abruptly: "Phil Royer drift up this way today?"

"*Did* he? He's in there now, so tanked he can hardly count his fingers. They say he's been asking to see me." Turk Exin, blocky of build and slow but sure-witted, had to tilt his head up to meet Remington's glance.

"Asking for you? Then the whole thing's working out better than I thought."

"What thing?" Turk's irritation was already falling away before a rising curiosity.

"Didn't you hear what happened?" Remington asked.

"How could I? We've been working that herd across to the railroad. The crew's loading tonight. By sunup, those critters ought to be on their way out."

"One of my line riders spotted the break in the fence at nine this morning," Remington said in seeming irrelevance. "By the time the boss and the rest of us got up there and found the herd gone, it was past eleven. Sloan sent the others on, following sign. Him and me headed straight for the line shack to see what had happened to Royer. We found him there, laying on the floor, his head bleeding, out cold."

"He might have stopped us last night," Turk explained. "I took care of him first."

"It looked like one of your jobs. Lucky you didn't kill him," Tentrock's foreman said in thinly veiled sarcasm. "As it turned out, it's the best thing that could have happened. The boss threw a bucket of water in his face and brought him to. Then he started asking questions, questions Royer didn't have the answers to."

"You didn't get me in here to tell me Jim Sloan's troubles," Turk said impatiently. "Let him raise all the hell he wants. The more the better."

"You don't get it, Turk. The man old Sloan raised hell with was Royer. It happened after we got back to the layout. On the way in, I mentioned a couple of things that made it look worse for Royer. The boss took him into the office alone. Ten minutes later, Royer skidded out of there on the seat of his pants. I saw the last of it. A man don't often take a beating like he took and soon forget it."

Turk drew in his breath sharply. "You mean Sloan thought Royer was in on the rustling? He whipped Royer, fired him?"

"Fired him and told him never to set foot inside Tentrock fence again unless he wanted a gun-whipping."

Turk whistled softly in sheer amazement.

"See now what it means, Turk? It's your chance to settle with Jim Sloan."

"By using Royer? Hell, he's no friend of mine."

"No, but after today he's through with Sloan."

A light of cunning edged into Turk's glance. "Do you reckon we can swing it?" he muttered. "I've waited twenty years for this, twenty years to settle things with the man that named me for a rustler, and ran me back into the hills."

Tentrock's foreman smiled thinly. "You ought to forget that story, Turk. You were rustling Sloan's stuff twenty years ago the same as you are now."

A sultry anger came to Turk's face. The truth obviously stung him. He could find no ready answer, and in a moment Remington was smoothing things over by saying: "Royer knows this country better than any man alive. With his help, we can run off enough stuff to put Sloan on the skids. Then, when the bank takes Tentrock over, you and me step in and buy the layout. . . ."

The ramrod's voice droned on insistently, pausing only to answer an occasional question of Turk's. At the end of a quarter hour, Turk, in a better frame of mind, nodded and said: "It listens nice, Sid. But what about Royer when we're through with him?"

Remington made a significant gesture, one in which his right hand fell to slap the holster at his thigh. Turk's eyes narrowed in hesitation and he said quickly: "That's your job, Sid."

Remington gave a soft laugh and walked over to pick up the black's reins and climb stiffly into the saddle. "You hold up your end of it end, I'll take care of mine, Turk," he said. "The herd will be there tomorrow night. Three hundred head, no guards. With luck, Royer and your crew can have it across the peaks by sunup the next morning." He frowned at a sudden inner thought. "How about the sheriff, Turk?"

"He gets a nice enough cut, don't he?" Turk stated, grinning.

"Then get started, Turk." Remington wheeled the black out into the alley and was gone a moment later.

When Turk took the passageway between the saloon and the adjoining building, he was smiling confidently. Out front, glancing along Hillton's steeply tilted street that ran along the cañon wall, he paused a moment to drag in a deep lungful of the crisp night air before he turned in at the Mile High's swing doors. He tried to erase the smile from his face.

Inside, business was tailing off for the night. It was past 11:00, and Max, the bartender, was momentarily idle over a game of pinochle with a customer at the bar's far end. At a table opposite the short bar, three men played a desultory game of stud under the glare of a lamp and in a fog of tobacco smoke.

Turk's glance settled on the sixth and last man in the room. This individual, middling tall and wide of shoulder, stood with elbows on the bar and one boot on the rail, his stance loose and plainly that of a man far gone in drink. His outfit was the ordinary range variety, Levi's and spurred boots, blue cotton shirt, and open vest. A wide-brimmed gray Stetson was tilted back on his sorrel-thatched head. Face and wrists were burned to a brick red. His face, lean and aquiline, might have been handsome but for the puffy bruise under his left eye and a sizeable swelling along that side of his jaw. The eyes were blue and now red-rimmed and bleary. His face was dark with a two-day growth of beard stubble. He wore a weapon in a holster hung low. He wasn't pleasant-looking.

He turned to face the doors as their double hinges bumped at Turk's entrance. When he saw who it was, a thin smile played across his face and he called: "C'mon, Turk. Have a drink!"

Then, when Turk had come warily across to stand alongside him at the bar, he laughed softly and said: "Two days ago if a man had told me I'd ever be buying a drink for Turk Exin, I'd have pushed his teeth down his throat."

Turk said: "Why the change, Royer?"

"Why the change?" Phil Royer gave the whiskey-thick laugh again. "Because today Jim Sloan put a name to me no man ever has. He gave me this bad eye and this jaw."

Turk smiled. "Jim Sloan's a big man. You'll learn sooner or later that he don't care who he tromps on. What was it about?"

"About you. Jim claimed I was in on that rustling job last night." Phil Royer's glance was direct, his eyes narrow-slitted as though he was having a hard time focusing them.

"Did anyone say I was in on that?" Turk evaded.

Royer turned away from him and pounded on the bar with an empty bottle that he'd stood at his elbow. He called for drinks, then turned to Turk to say: "What the hell do I care if you run off that Tentrock stuff last night, if you've run off all the others Sloan's lost these last two years? Turk, I never saw your side of this argument until today." He poured two drinks from the bottle the apron slid along the counter and raised his own glass. "Well, here's to Jim Sloan's poor health."

They drank. As Phil Royer set his glass down, he said: "I'm up here looking for a job. Can you give me one?"

Turk shook his head. "I'd sooner have a wildcat bedded down in my calf corral."

"I mean it, Turk. You hate Jim Sloan's guts, always have. So do I, now. It's all right with me if you can rustle him into the poorhouse, better if I can help you do it."

Turk poured himself another drink, cuffed it off. "I'm thinking of doing that very thing," he stated.

Royer's glance sharpened. "The hell you say! When?"

"When I get ready."

"Then take me on. I'll help you do it."

Turk shook his head. "Unh-uh. I'm playing it too close to the belt to take a chance like that, Phil."

"To hell with the chance you're taking," Phil Royer drawled in his whiskey-thick voice. "You need me. For instance, I could take every critter in that Tentrock hill pasture through their fence in broad daylight and a man a mile away wouldn't know they were on the move. I could. . . ."

"I've got all the help I need on Tentrock," Turk cut in. "Someone over there lets me know which fence isn't being guarded, where the herds are. Between us, we've managed to keep Sloan remembering how he pushed me off good grass and back into those hills twenty years ago. Sooner or later I'll even that score."

"Who's your man on Tentrock?" Phil Royer asked bluntly, his glance sharpening.

Turk smiled broadly. "How much did Sloan pay you to come here and ask me that?" He spoke before he thought. He saw instantly the quick anger that flared alive in Phil Royer's eyes. Royer pushed back from the bar and let his hands fall to his sides. Turk went pale at the threat behind that gesture, hastened to say: "Easy, Phil. Reckon I didn't mean that." He saw the tenseness gradually go out of Royer, and in his genuine relief he made the decision that here was a man he could trust. "About that job, Phil. You really want it?"

The bleakness of a moment ago remained imprinted on Phil Royer's face. He said savagely: "Why the hell would I be here if I didn't?"

That settled it with Turk. He insisted on buying another two rounds of drinks, and meanwhile their talk drifted along the channels Sid Remington had earlier outlined. The whiskey in his guts sharpened Turk's wits and seemed to dull Phil Royer's. After their first understanding, that he was hired and would ride with Turk's crew, Royer lost interest in everything but the bottle.

As he took his second drink, his knees buckled a little and he swayed heavily against the bar.

Turk saw that and said: "Better go easy on the fire water, Phil. We have a twelve-mile ride ahead of us tonight."

Royer shook his head loosely. "Not me. I'll be out in the morning. I got a bed all picked out in the stable loft. Have 'nother drink, Turk."

Turk's hand reached the bottle before Royer's did. "Let's call it quits, Phil. If you're working tomorrow, you can't be riding off a hang-over."

The cowpuncher shrugged indifferently, pushed out from the bar, and would have fallen if Turk's hand hadn't steered him. They left the Mile High that way, Royer's arm about Turk's shoulder and most of his weight against the other man. Turk was patient on the way to the feed barn, twice talking Royer out of going back to the saloon. Finally, after boosting him up the ladder into the loft, Turk saw his new crew member safely bedded down in the hay. In a quarter minute Royer was snoring. Turk left.

Phil Royer listened until Turk's solid boot tread had faded out into the stillness down the plank walk on the street. Then he sat up and shook his head to clear it, for the four drinks he'd taken with Turk had left him a little groggy. He unbuttoned his shirt and took out a flat, large-necked canteen. This canteen and the spittoon along the Mile High's bar contained most of the whiskey from the quart bottle he'd pretended to empty down his throat this afternoon and tonight. He corked the canteen and buried it in the hay, and then soundlessly climbed back down the loft ladder, a completely sober man.

Five minutes later he had sneaked his saddle off the pole at the rear of the barn and his sorrel horse from the corral out behind, moving so quietly that the snores of the hostler, asleep in his office in front, continued unbroken.

Once out of sight of Hillton's few late-winking lights, he lifted the sorrel to a quick canter and followed the trail that led down out of the cañon. An hour's steady going put him well out onto the flats through Tentrock's fence. As he rode up a sparsely wooded slope toward the line shack where this morning he had been found lying unconscious, he made out Jim Sloan's bulky shape in the shadow of the low-hanging eaves.

When Phil had reined in alongside the rancher, he saw at once the set, bleak expression on the man's face. He said: "The word got there, Jim. Turk's talked to me. I'm his right bower now. It looks like it worked."

Jim Sloan seemed strangely unmoved by this news. He said flatly: "Phil, I've had my eye on every man at the layout since noon, since I kicked you out. The only one who could have carried the word to Turk was Sid Remington."

"Then my guess was right?"

The rancher let out a weary sigh. "Looks like it, although I'll need more proof than this. Sid left at five tonight, saying he was on his way to town to see a girl. It's a hell of a thing to believe of a man that's turned in the work for me Sid has."

"But it's staring you in the face, boss."

"I know, I know," Sloan said impatiently. "When does it happen, Phil? Is it like you said it would be . . . Turk made you the proposition to help drive off my herds?"

Phil nodded. "Tomorrow night. Turk seemed pretty sure there'd be three or four hundred head in the hill pasture. He seemed to think they wouldn't be under guard."

"The crew'll be there tomorrow night, not the herd," Jim Sloan said ominously. As an afterthought, he added: "Sorry I hit you so hard that last time this morning. But Sid was watching. I had to make it look real."

Phil's hand went to his swollen jaw and he grinned wryly. "It hurt right then. But I'd do it again if it pried your eyes open to who's helping Turk."

Their talk drifted on for another five minutes, Jim Sloan's anger blunt and ominous in comparison to his usual good humor. Shortly they put their ponies down the slope of the hill away from the shack. A mile farther on they parted, Sloan riding toward Tentrock's headquarters, Phil striking in toward the hills.

A lone light in Tentrock's bunkhouse was pinpointing the night's distance when Sid Remington happened to remember that this morning he'd left his brier pipe in the line shack where they had found Phil Royer. He glanced upward at the wheeling stars and judged the time to be close to midnight. Since he was wide-awake and hungry for a really satisfying smoke to take the place of the cigarettes he'd used all day, he decided to make the swing north and get the pipe before he turned in.

Three quarters of an hour later, he saw the two riders coming down along the slope from the shack barely in time to rein behind a screening of scrub cedar and keep from being discovered. He was out of the saddle in an instant, his hand clamped over the black's nostrils to keep the animal from whickering and giving away his presence.

Phil Royer and Jim Sloan rode by less than forty feet out from the cedars. Recognizing them, Remington had a moment or two of sheer panic. Finally, when they had ridden out of hearing, his pulse settled back to its normal beat and he spent a long quarter hour reshaping certain of his thoughts.

Knowing what he must do, he sloped into the saddle again and headed back into the hills with Turk Exin's layout as his destination.

II

The sun's red-orange disk was topping the rolling horizon to the east late the next afternoon as Phil and Turk Exin left the trail that twisted down out of the foothills and rode straight south toward Tentrock's fence. Turk had been sullen and uncommunicative in the two hours since Phil had ridden out from Hillton to the Block E. He seemed nervous over what was happening, keyed up to this one night that was going to give him a revenge he'd waited twenty years to take.

"Better be swinging west, hadn't we?" Phil said to Turk ten minutes later, and started reining his sorrel aside.

Turk was a few paces behind him. "We'd better keep going straight on!" Turk's voice grated harshly in a way that made Phil turn quickly to face him. Turk had a Colt fisted in his hand. It was lined at Phil's chest.

Phil pulled in on the reins and then slowly lifted his hands above his head. In the three-second silence that followed, Turk's face took on a down-lipped smile. At length he said: "Go ahead, make your play, Royer."

Long-trained wariness made Phil keep his hands where they were, for Turk's .45 was cocked and there was a finger on the trigger. "What's the idea, Turk?" he drawled.

"The idea's that Sid ran onto you and Jim Sloan up at line shack last night."

Into the silence that followed, Phil drawled: "Well, get it over with, Turk."

Turk's smile broadened. He shook his head. "Unh-uh. You're coming along, just in case Jim Sloan shows up." He thrust out his left hand. "I'll take your hardware. Better move slow."

When he had thrust Phil's six-gun through the waistband of his trousers, he motioned ahead with his .45. "Keep headed the way you were. We're meeting the crew along the east fence."

A quarter hour's riding made it all plain to Phil Royer. By

that time they had sighted the unshapely, sprawling mass of the herd that was being gathered along Tentrock's east fence. Dusk was coming on fast, yet even in this uncertain light Phil saw that the broad east pasture had been gutted of animals that were already working on through a wide gap in the wire, choused by a dozen of Turk's men. He realized grimly that Jim Sloan no longer had a chance. Tentrock's crew was five miles to the west, set for an ambush that would never take place; while here, almost within sight of Tentrock's headquarters, the very life blood of the outfit was being drained in one quick thrust that meant complete and utter ruin to Jim Sloan. And there was nothing Phil could do about it.

Phil's feeling of helplessness was increased when they rode in on the herd and Sid Remington came out to meet them. The Tentrock ramrod stopped twenty feet away, eyeing Phil with a smug smile.

"Like it, Royer?" he queried in cutting sarcasm.

"If it works, it's good," Phil said.

Remington's glance swiveled to Turk. "Sloan thought he was playing it safe. Had the sheriff out this morning and put me under arrest. Our friend took a hundred dollars of my money to let me go on the way in to jail. Let's make this fast, Turk. I'll send across a man to help you watch Royer."

Phil's two guards, Turk and a dour-visaged killer packing two guns, didn't let him out of their sight as the quick dusk faded into complete darkness broken only by the light of myriad stars. At times they rode close to him; at others, they lagged behind, yet always close enough to let them see any move he made. The herd worked north and into the hills, and three hours saw it winding its thick stem up the twisting trail of a high-walled cañon. In all this time, Phil saw Sid Remington only once, yet he heard the man's voice shouting orders from far back in the drag.

That cañon offered Phil his first slim chance. It took him a long time to see it, but in the end he was ready and knew what he must do. The cañon, narrowing as it climbed through the foothills toward the peaks, placed the riders close to the very animals Turk and his companion were riding with their prisoner in the swing position, who now was almost upon the two rustlers that were working the herd ahead of them.

Twice in five minutes, Phil was close enough to one of the rustlers' horses that his stirrup touched the neighboring pony's flank. The third time this happened, he kicked off his boot from the stirrup and hunched over, throwing his long frame from the saddle in a quick roll.

He was down behind his sorrel before the first gun, Turk's, spoke in an explosion that ripped up along the cañon's corridor. He landed on his feet and dived in between the rustlers' horses, racing forward toward the herd.

Three lunging steps more carried him in between two plodding steers. A second shot bent the air and a bullet plonked into the steer alongside him, and the animal went down with a wild, frightened bawl. Hunched over, he ran deeper into the herd while other guns spoke, and Turk's angry shout summoned Sid Remington.

Phil was halfway through the herd, side-stepping, dodging the four-foot spread of steers' horns, before the nervous fright brought on by the gunfire behind spooked the animals. By that time the riders were out of sight in the blackness behind. He came erect, and, shoving, fighting his way, finally gained the far margin of the herd.

As he stepped clear, a rider's shape rushed up out of the blackness, calling: "Where's your jughead? What's going on back there?"

Phil saw instantly that he hadn't been recognized. He ran across to the rider calling: "Get back! They're coming this way!"

"Who?" the rider shouted, sliding his pony to a stop and bending low in the saddle to catch Phil's answer.

Phil caught him that way, off-balance. He struck the man's jaw with all the strength of his flat-muscled body behind his knotted fist. He caught the rider's Colt as it fell. He wasted precious time in dragging the man's inert body high up into the rocks along the cañon wall and removing his gun belt. Then, leaping into the saddle, he headed for the point of the herd, thumbing three quick shots into the air to add to the panic of the fear-crazed animals.

Half a minute put him within sight of two point riders who were vainly trying to work back against the onrush of the herd. He fell in with them, unrecognized, and ten seconds later brought his Colt down solidly on the Stetson of the first man. The second saw his blow strike and wheeled and palmed up a six-gun. Phil's weapon bucked in his hand and his bullet drove the rider out of the saddle before the other's draw was completed.

He reloaded as he reined on ahead of the lead steers. He emptied the .45 at the leaders and succeeded in turning one or two of them back. Animals behind milled after the leaders and abruptly the cañon bottom was filled to brimming with solidly packed steers fighting to put distance between them and that insistently speaking gun up ahead.

Shouts sounded above the hoof thunder far to the rear now, and Phil smiled grimly at the thought of the riders trapped in their swing positions, faced with an unforgiving mass of animals behind and more pushing at them from the front. He loaded and emptied his gun twice again, making sure that the herd was circling back upon itself. Then a rattle of gunfire far back told him that riders there were fighting for their lives against the gathering stampede.

He spotted one rider climbing his horse up a break in the

wall. He laid his sights on the rider and sent two snap shots, and saw that the shape in the saddle went down.

Suddenly, from behind him, a six-gun spoke and hot lead laid a concussion of air along his face. He reined wildly aside, turning as his pony lunged. Sid Remington was barely ten feet away, his Colt lining down once again.

Phil threw himself from the saddle. Remington's second shot burned the flesh along his upper left arm. He lit, spraddle-legged, his weapon swinging into line. Instinct timed the smooth play of hand and arm as he thumbed three thought-quick shots at the Tentrock ramrod. He saw Remington lurch awkwardly, come erect again. His next bullet made the ramrod's gaunt frame jerk convulsively. Then Remington was down, hanging onto the reins until his shying black horse broke them from his death grip.

Later, Phil climbed his pony up a stretch of sheer-tilted rock and moved out of the way of the herd that once more turned back on itself. This time the animals thundered straight up the cañon in a relentless charge that nothing could have stopped. But now there were no riders to stop them, and as the hoof thunder died into the distance, there were no voices, no rattle of gunfire, to break the stillness. All at once Phil did hear something that kept him where he was, screened by a maze of outcroppings up along the foot of the wall. It was the slurring beat of horses on the move. It grew louder, and in another two minutes a bunch of riders swung into sight below.

Phil lined his sights at the nearest man, ready to cut him if he was discovered. Then, miraculously, Jim Sloan's voice shouted from out of the group: "Royer!" There was a moment's silence, and then the rancher spoke to the others in a softer, worried tone. "Do you reckon he was trampled like the rest?"

Phil came out of his crouch, calling: "Here, Jim!"

When he was alongside Sloan a minute afterward, the relief

mirrored on the rancher's face was clear and unmistakable. "We heard the guns and came up here hell for leather, Phil," the rancher said. "It looked like you were gone with the rest, what's left of 'em." He waved an arm downcañon. "We counted six bodies, one that looks like it might have been Turk. I had Remington arrested, so that's taken care. . . ."

"Remington's lying right over there, Jim," Phil cut in.

Jim Sloan's look was one of incredulity until Phil told him about the sheriff. The rancher said ominously: "It won't take us long to put him in his own jail." Some inner thought relaxed the grim set of his face then, and he turned to Phil, crying: "Tentrock's in the clear now, with her best years ahead! I'm a poor hand at thanking a man, Phil, but would Remington's job suit you?"

"You've bought yourself a new straw boss, Jim," Phil said.

* * * * *

Treasure Freight

* * * * *

This story was submitted to Popular Publications by Jon Glidden's agent in June, 1948. The pulp magazines were coming to an end. "Colt-Cure for Woolly Fever," which would be published in Popular Publications' *Big-Book Western* (2/49), would be the last Peter Dawson submission ever made to this publisher. "Treasure Freight" was the penultimate submission and it was bought for 3¢ a word and published under the title "Boss of Back-Shoot Claim" in *New Western* (11/48). "Colt-Cure for Wooly Fever" has been collected in Peter Dawson's *Ghost of the Chinook* (Five Star, 2004) and is available in a full-cast dramatization with music and sound effects in *Great American Westerns: Volume Three* from Graphic Audio. "Treasure Freight" has had its title and text restored for this first appearance in book form.

I

There were a lot of things the letter could have told me. It could have mentioned the Sunbeam, the gold, or Thomas Bemis, the man we were going in to work for. But no, not a word about any of this.

Instead, it told about the way a trail climbed a certain rim below Lode. At the time I'd thought how queer it was, Ed wasting words on a thing like that. The same went for what he'd written about some girl up there. I laid both to his plain cussedness, his wanting me to know he was boss, and that he had things well enough in hand to spend time noticing females. All this even though the superintendent had given him to understand he was to stick strictly to the job and that I was in full charge.

Anyway, now that I was looking out through the pines across this narrow valley and could see the rim and the trail, I began to understand why Ed had used up words on it. Like he'd said, a man would never have a prayer of climbing it by day without being seen. And I was trying to get to Lode without anyone knowing about it—anyone but Ed.

While giving the trail the once over, I remember wondering how important that other worthless-seeming item in his letter might turn out to be, this girl he'd mentioned. But then I forgot her as I looked out on that wall of rimrock, climbing squarely up for maybe six hundred feet.

The creek that came down the cañon above spilled off the

rim's near end in the prettiest falls you ever saw, with the last of the sun playing on it and a rainbow arched out of the spray hanging over the big pool below. And the trail that climbed those hundreds of feet looked narrow and mean, and made you believe all you'd ever heard about how crazy men can go over gold.

The Lode diggings lay along the cañon above, so naturally they'd found a way up this wall—the only way. You could see how they had followed a fault line to make the first long traverse from the valley bottom, probably blasting it out with Giant powder.

Then after that stretch, all of a mile, they had switched back and made the top by blowing the rock out in another straight line, steep as all get out. Lay a V on its side and there'd be your road up the rim.

There was nothing for me to do but kill time till dark, so I rode on back through the jack pine till I found a grassy coulée. There I took the saddle off the gelding, poor devil, and staked him out to feed while I scouted some cedar and cooked the first decent hot meal I'd been able to fix in two whole days.

If it hadn't been for drinking a whole fry-pan batch of coffee, I'd have gone to sleep then and there. I was as played out as the roan. He'd been on the go steadily since late last night, and me for two days and a night, all because Ed Demmler had said to get the hell up here fast. Something was up.

Once, while I was eating, I heard some shouting out toward the rim, and walked on up so as to look off through the pines to the trail. A muleskinner was making the bend over there, leading a string of twelve big mules so heavily packed they staggered. And damned if one didn't fall from that ledge above the turn while I was watching.

He snapped his rope, some rock came down with him, and for a second it looked like he'd catch himself on the ledge below.

But no, he went on down and I heard him hit clear across where I was, a good quarter of a mile away. Then you could hear the muleskinner's cussing real plain. I picked up a new word or two.

That kind of woke me up, so by the time it was dark and I had forked the roan across to the trail up, I didn't take a chance on staying in the saddle. If it hadn't been dark, I'd probably have crawled all the way. As it turned out, I did crawl across the stretch where the unlucky mule had brought down some fair-size boulders.

I was wondering how they could keep the trail open in winter with the freezes and thaws loosening the ledges and such. The roan had a hard time of it. Part of the time we were under overhangs that blotted out the stars. With the roan so played out we took a good hour to make it to the top, fair time for those two steep miles. We didn't meet anybody, which was the luck I'd been hoping for. Later I was to learn no one used the trail after dark. Too many men had cashed in trying it.

Follow the trail up to where the cut narrows, Ed had said, and you'll come onto the ruin of a cabin with a caved-in roof. I'll be waiting there for you beginning three nights from now.

This was the fourth night, which meant Ed's hair-trigger temper would be on edge over my being late. Or maybe he hadn't really meant the third night, knowing how slow the mails must be and only wanting to see me wear myself out covering more than two hundred miles.

By now you may have started thinking I wasn't so fond of Ed Demmler. I wasn't. He was lazy, he took whiskey sometimes when being sober was part of the job, and anything in skirts could catch his eye. He made no real friends. He was cold-blooded as they came. He had a tongue tight as a pounded dowel, and he was one man I'd hate to go up against with a gun. All in all he was the best man we could find to go in first and size up the Lode trouble. So I had him sent in. He'd been there ten days now. He should know something.

Well, I found the cabin all right. And Ed Demmler was waiting for me. Inside. In the far corner by a mound of dried mud plaster that had fallen off the chimney. The moon had just topped the wall of the cañon to the southeast, and it lit that end of the cabin enough to see everything clearly. The dark stain under his head. Everything.

Ed was dead.

A shotgun—buckshot, it looked like—had ripped his face apart. Or maybe a wolf or coyote had been working him over. Anyway, you couldn't have told it was him. His pockets were turned inside out and the only way I knew him was by his shirt.

It was flannel, bright red and double-breasted, with mother-of-pearl buttons. He had paid $3 for it and he'd been proud of it in the same way he was proud of his matched pair of Navy Colt .44s. He was still wearing the .44s. Before I carried him on up through the trees and caved in a rotting ledge along the creek over him, I took his guns and wrapped them in my blanket roll.

If I hadn't been so riled, at a boil so deep down, I wouldn't have been able to lug him all that distance. For a time, until I needed my wind, I remember cussing the way the muleskinner had cussed out there on the trail earlier. Though I'd privately decided long ago that Ed would come to a bad end, nothing about the way he'd died seemed right. He'd had no chance. It didn't come to me till after the ledge had fallen down over him what all this meant for me.

That sort of took the steam out of me, and I stood there watching the dust settle over his sorry grave in the moonlight, knowing he had been a careful man and realizing how careful I'd have to be unless I wanted to wind up where he was. The hard part about it all—about going ahead with the job—was that I didn't have one damned thing to go on. Ed's letter had said next to nothing. Now it was just the same as though I was coming in on the thing cold. Nothing at all.

Well, there didn't seem any choice but to go straight ahead, so I went back to the gelding by the cabin, and climbed onto him and went on up the trail. All the thinking I did during the ten minutes it took me to bring the lights of Lode into sight netted me exactly nothing.

It was a poor excuse for a town. Except for the lanterns of the shaft houses glowing up both slopes above, there wasn't any reason for it being where it was. Here the cañon was so narrow the tents and tar-paper-and-slab shacks didn't have any place to sit except on the inclines.

The few feet of level ground along the creek had become the street, with here and there single planks bridging the water for foot traffic. There were only two real buildings in the settlement, and neither was built solidly enough to have suited a homesteader for a barn. Both were saloons, of course, and on the way in I counted four more establishments, all tents, advertising whiskey for sale.

Up toward the center of town a bunch of coal-oil flares lit the street that was alive with men swarming through the mud, some of them wading the creek instead of using the planks to cross it. From somewhere came the tinny strumming of a piano—Lord knows how they had got the thing up the rim trail—and it surprised me to see three or four women, percentage girls probably, when I looked in at one of the saloon tents.

There wasn't much sense in putting things off, even if I was so dog-tired. So when a man cut across the street in front of me, I reined on over alongside him and asked: "Mister, where's the Sunbeam?"

He tilted his head, pointing with his chin up the south slope. "Them lights farthest up."

I thanked him and went on, my hat pulled low so that no one would particularly notice me, threading the gelding through the heavy foot traffic and now and then making way for a man on a mule or a scrubby pony.

At the upper end of the street there was a rutted road swinging off up the south slope, so I took it. Halfway up that climb the roan stopped and refused to budge any farther. I led him off into the trees, tied him, and went on afoot. Talk about winded—I surely was when I'd climbed those last three hundred yards.

It was the Sunbeam, right enough. There was a slab fence around the shaft house and a couple other buildings, and the fence was topped by three tight strands of barb-wire. On the gate was a big sign lit by a lantern hanging over it:

PRIVATE PROPERTY, KEEP OUT, THIS MEANS YOU!
SUNBEAM GOLD INC.

The sign read like it meant business, and as I walked up on it, I was wondering how to get in. I didn't have to wonder long. I was maybe thirty feet off when the gate swung back and a tall, lanky jasper holding a carbine eased into the opening.

"You must be lost, stranger," he said.

He could hear how hard I was breathing, so I let him listen to that a few seconds while I got my wind and thought up something to say. Finally I grinned and told him: "I was beginning to think so. But now I see I'm not. They told me there was work up here."

He had a face like a faro dealer's, one that told you nothing. I saw his eyes drop and take in my boots, then my holster, finally my hat. "Ever swing a single jack?" he asked.

I shook my head. "I could learn how."

"Ever do any muckin'?"

"Only around a barn."

Now he shook his head. "Not a chance," he drawled. "We're

hirin' nothin' but hard-rock men."

"Look, friend," I came back at him real easy. "I come all this way for a try at my luck. I need a stake." I had a thought then that made me decide on something else. "You got mules to look after?"

"Sure. We pay a kid two-bits a day for that. Now. . . ."

All of a sudden he turned at a sound behind him and his look changed, became respectful. He touched his hat, said— " 'Evenin', folks."—and reached out to swing the gate wide open. Then I could see the team of blacks and the buggy right behind him, and the man and woman sitting in the buggy.

The buggy lamps were lit and maybe it was because of my seeing that the woman was really a girl, a downright beautiful girl, that I didn't move out of the center of the road as the blacks came out the gate and trotted down at me. I must have been staring pretty openly at the girl, because as the team stopped just in front of me, the man beside her said gruffly: "You, there! Move!"

I started to move. Then I really saw him for the first time and stopped. He was big, even bigger than I was, and his outfit looked expensive and clean, too clean for any ordinary man living in a mining camp. So I knew right away he must be Tom Bemis, owner of the Sunbeam, the man I'd been sent up here to work with. This was as good a time as any to make his acquaintance.

"Mister," I began, "they told me down below you'd always take on a good man." I nodded to the guard at the gate. "He claims you won't."

Bemis had been glowering at me. Now his expression eased to disinterest. "He's right. We're hiring no one but miners."

Real quick I got another idea and, letting my right hand rub the thonged-down holster at my thigh, I drawled: "You wouldn't have any other sort of work?"

It was the girl, not Bemis, who answered that in a roundabout way by looking at him and saying softly: "Tom, he might be just the one."

A look I didn't understand any more than what she'd said passed between them. The only thing I gathered was that I'd guessed right on his being Bemis, for she'd called him Tom.

Then he was saying, to me: "Maybe I could give you something, after all. Know where the President Grant is?"

"No. But I can find out."

"It's the next mine up the cañon. Meet me there at nine tomorrow morning." And he lifted the reins.

As I was moving farther out of the way, the girl looked at me again and, still speaking to Bemis, asked: "Wouldn't tonight do just as well?"

"Why all the hurry, Ruth?"

I heard her sigh. "Simply because I want to get it settled." Looking straight at me, she added: "Could you come across tonight? To the President Grant?"

"Surely could," I answered.

The blacks started on, and as the buggy passed me, she looked down and called: "As soon as you can get there!" The buggy was gone then, swallowed by the blackness of the thick timber down the road.

I stood looking after it, wondering what I was letting myself in for, when the guard spoke abruptly behind me. "Better stay away from it, stranger."

I turned to face him. "From what?"

"The job she'll offer you."

"What's that to be?"

He halfway smiled, probably showing as much amusement as he ever did. "You'll find out," was his cryptic answer. "Only take my word for it now, and turn it down."

He'd had his say and now stepped over to the gate and swung

it shut. I heard a bar drop on the inside and right then I was feeling that this place was just about as friendly as my meeting with Ed had indicated it would be.

II

Walking back down to the roan, I didn't have much luck putting sense to what had happened, except that the girl was anxious to get something done, something Bemis saw no point in hurrying. I hadn't particularly taken to him, maybe because I envied him the girl.

He looked like the kind that would want to wash his hands every time they touched dirt, and I wondered why he'd let his pride put him to the expense and foolishness of using a new buggy and fine team over these roads even if he did own the Sunbeam. I was acquainted with several prosperous men, mostly ranchers, yet not a one of them ever put on airs and, one and all, they weren't afraid of work or of soiling their clothes.

Back down in town again I found a corral and left the roan there, hiring the best horse on the lot, a spavined gray, to carry me up to the President Grant. The road up to it was easier than the other, but this nag I was forking paid no attention to the spur and took his own good time. So I arrived at the mine maybe twenty minutes after Bemis and the girl.

The President Grant was different from the Sunbeam. No fence around it, no shaft house—later I learned it was a drift operation—only a couple of huts of peeled aspen poles. One of the huts was showing a light, so I headed toward it.

As I was coming aground at the rail in front of it, I could hear voices. One was Bemis's, there was a second man's, then there was the girl's. You could tell even without understanding what they were saying that it was some kind of argument.

It came to me then that I might do worse than eavesdrop, so I eased in quietly on the door and listened in time to hear the

167

last of something Bemis was saying.

". . . don't want to hire someone we can't trust. What do we know about him?"

It was the girl who answered: "I can judge men, Tom. We can trust this one. Besides, his trustworthiness doesn't enter into it."

Then this other voice spoke up. "What would your father say to it, miss?"

"Dad respects my judgment, Matt. Didn't he tell me to do what I could? Good heavens, things couldn't be worse than they are."

"Now, Ruth," Bemis drawled smoothly. "Let's think straight on this. We know Wells Fargo's sending a couple men in here to investigate. Let's wait before we try anything."

And one's already cashed in, I was saying to myself as the girl burst out: "Wait! Haven't we waited long enough? We're just inviting a gang of cut-throats to help themselves."

"You wouldn't have to worry about the gold if you'd use the safe in my office," Bemis said.

"Your men can be bought off and you know it, Tom."

All they were saying made sense to me, for I knew what had been going on around there these past two months. There seemed no special point in listening any longer, so I backed away from the door a few steps, coughed, and came in on it again, stomping the mud from my boots. The voice that was speaking, the second man's, broke off as I knocked.

Bemis opened the door. "Come on in," he said in a sort of high and mighty way, like he might have told someone who had just polished his boots to keep the change.

I went on in, took off my hat, and the girl said: "Thank you for coming. I'm Ruth Vance. My father owns the mine. This—" she nodded to the second man, short, thick-built, with bushy brown hair and eyebrows—"is our foreman, Matt White. You probably know Mister Bemis."

I said—"Howdy."—to White and nodded to Bemis, and then, to cinch it, told the girl: "This is a piece of luck for me, miss, picking up work."

She had been eyeing me with some interest. But now something I'd said made her look uneasy and she glanced at Bemis. "You tell him, Tom."

Bemis said—"Let's all sit down."—so we moved across the small room to a table and took chairs. The only other furnishings in the room were a cot and a second table heaped with a mess of papers and ledgers.

Matt White offered Bemis, then me, cigars, and when we had our smokes going, Bemis asked straight out: "What's your name, stranger?"

"Slim," I told him. Which was the truth as far as it went.

He smiled crookedly, as though he was making something of my not giving him more name than that to go on. "That'll do good enough," he said smugly, and his pale eyes were going over me as he put another question: "Slim, how would you like to earn a hundred dollars for a day's work?"

I whistled softly, looking from him to the girl, thinking to read more in her face than in his. But she was only watching me, eager for my answer.

"That's a lot of money," I said. "What's the catch?"

"There's no catch. It's exactly what I say. A hundred dollars for a day's work."

"What kind of work?"

"Packing a load of dust out to the railroad."

"Gold?"

Bemis smiled thinly. "That's a fool question, Slim. Of course it's gold."

I thought a moment. "Why such high pay?"

"Because," Bemis answered, smooth as silk, "you'll probably be killed on your way out."

169

I took in a deep drag of air and let it go so it made some noise. Maybe I was smiling as I said: "Now that's laying the cards on the line. Suppose I make it, and don't get killed?"

"Then you get the hundred."

"Suppose I keep on going with the gold?"

"You won't."

He meant that. It was easy to tell. He was cocksure, maybe threatening, and as we eyed each other, the girl put in: "Tom, that's a ridiculous way to explain this. Tell him exactly what he'll be doing. And why."

Bemis took a hefty drag at his cigar and squinted at me through the smoke. "Slim, you'd be signing on with a hard-luck outfit. There are seven operations here, all working gold. The President Grant and my Sunbeam are the only two of the seven taking the yellow stuff out in anything like pure form. The rest mill theirs and freight out concentrates. They've been let strictly alone. We're the only two in trouble."

"Trouble?" I had to ask it, even if I knew what he meant.

"Trouble and plenty of it," he went on. "Not an ounce of gold has gone out of either this mine or the Sunbeam the last two months. Gone all the way, that is. I don't know how it happened that Vance and I decided to ship together. Anyway, we did, probably because it was easier to hire one batch of guards instead of two. We've made two tries. The first shipment I had insured by Wells Fargo. It was a four-man train using pack mules. It was caught on that trail you must've come in on along the rim. Two men were shot by rifles from below, the third fell over the cliff trying to get away, the fourth somehow got back to the top and into town here."

When he paused, I asked: "And the gold?"

He lifted his hands off the table, let them fall again. That was all he did.

"How about the second try?"

"Almost the same story. Wells Fargo paid off on the insurance, then sent men in to take out the second shipment. Miss Vance's father went along. There were eight men as I remember. Two went on ahead of the rest and down the trail and forted up below the rim. That made just two less to be dealt with. The shooting this time began at the head of the trail just as the mules went into it. Shooting from above and below. The mules were panicked and every last one went over. One man was seriously wounded. Sam Vance. He's been in bed here ever since."

I looked at the girl. "Sorry, miss." Then I asked: "What about the gold this second time?"

Bemis shook his head. "Gone, like the rest. For two hours, until dark, the pair of men we'd sent below were nailed down right where they were by rifles shooting from the timber down there. Right after dark they heard a lot of moving around over by the cliff. They wasted some lead trying to scare off whoever it was. But by the next morning, when we got down there, the dead mules were stripped and we recovered about a tenth of the shipment."

He'd told the story pretty straight. Or rather he'd told as much of it as the superintendent had told me back at Wells Fargo's divisional office. So I was revising my opinion of Bemis slightly upward as I said: "So now you want me to be the sucker and try and make it on my own when eight men couldn't?"

"That's about it," he admitted. "Only those other times the whole camp knew the shipment was being made. This time no one'll know."

I looked from him to White to the girl. "Four of us know it to start with."

His face colored and he straightened in his chair. "You've got a salty tongue, stranger," he drawled.

"I've also got a hide I aim to keep in one piece." I rose from the table. "It's no dice, gents. But thanks for the offer."

It was the girl's hurt and baffled expression that kept me from moving to the door right away. Looking squarely at me, she went pale with what looked like anger. Then, in a hushed voice, she asked: "What are we to do?"

"Wait on Wells Fargo," Bemis told her.

It dawned on me then that Bemis was really satisfied with the way things were developing, and I had a queer hunch that for some reason he didn't want the girl's gold taken out. And when he went on speaking, my hunch that he felt that way was even stronger.

"Look, Ruth," he said, "why not give up on this? You don't want to bother your father with this trouble. There seems nothing to be done about it. Turn your gold over to me and trust me with it. Or do the other thing I suggested."

The glance she gave him wasn't the kind I'd want a girl to give me if she thought a lot of me. She was sore, sure, but there wasn't any softness in her eyes. "I'll wait on Wells Fargo," she said.

"Don't you trust me, Ruth?"

"I do. But it's not a matter of trust. One day you'll decide to take your gold out. And ours, if I give it to you. If Dad and I should lose it, we'd have to sell the mine. And we won't do that because it's all we have in the world."

"You could own half the Sunbeam by saying the right word, Ruth. You could own it tonight."

Her face took on color now and she looked away from him, not saying anything.

So that's how the wind blows, I was thinking as I went to the door. I asked—"You wouldn't have any other work, would you?"—and Bemis only smiled, shaking his head. So I got out of there right away.

III

It took me maybe a quarter hour to ride the hired jughead down the road a piece, tie him well off in the trees, and hoof it on back. I was working on around the cabin that showed the lights when Bemis and the girl came out and stood for a minute by the buggy.

The moonlight was strong enough to let me see her turn her cheek to him when he put his arms around her, and by the time he was heading down the road in the buggy, I was wondering why she'd act that way with a man who'd asked her to marry him. I was wondering about some other things, too.

But wondering didn't help much, so I watched her go back to the cabin, open the door, and stand there a minute, talking to her foreman, Matt White. Then she walked across to the second cabin. A light came on in a window there in a few seconds and I knew then that she and her father must be living in it. So I hurried on around the other one and went down there.

When the door opened to my soft knock, she was standing there with her pale hair flowing down about her shoulders instead of braided and wound around her head as it had been before. She was even prettier this way, so maybe that was why my voice sort of balled up on me as I spoke barely above a whisper: "Miss, I've got to talk with you."

Afterward, I couldn't figure quite why she was so trusting. We could have stood there at the door to talk, or she could even have stepped outside. Instead, she opened the door wide, telling me: "We'll have to be quiet. Dad's not too well tonight."

Once inside, I glanced at the window. "Would you mind pulling the shade?"

She looked startled but did as I said, not questioning it. So I decided right then to tell her all I had to tell. And to begin with I took the wallet from my back pocket and handed her a card—

the same sort of card the killer must have found on Ed. It simply said I was in the employ of Wells Fargo as an investigator, gave my name, Robert Spane, and asked any and all law enforcement officers to assist me in any way possible.

You should have seen her eyes right then. They were the kind of blue I once saw in a pillar of ice frozen over the cap of an artesian down San Luis Valley way, only they were warm-looking, not cold. Now they were opened wide, and her look was like a kid's being told his lost pup had been found.

Real softly she said: "I just couldn't believe you were the kind who wouldn't help."

Well, if she'd asked me to go against a grizzly with one hand strapped to my belt, I'd've done it just then. All I could think to say was: "Maybe I can't do much, miss. But I'm here to try."

"You'll do it. You'll find out what's behind all this." Then a kind of unsettling softness came to her eyes and she murmured: "You're tired, aren't you? Would you like some coffee?"

"Coffee would sure go down good."

Her kitchen was nothing but a lean-to built onto the back of the cabin, but it turned out to be one of the most comfortable home-like rooms I was ever in. She closed the door—and without being told hung a blanket over the window—and, while the fire was catching in the stove and the pot coming to a boil, we talked.

Her father was in the next room, she said, asleep. He'd got a bullet through his leg and at first the wound hadn't seemed bad. But infection had set in and he'd had a rough time of it. Now he was better, and going to get well. Meantime, she'd kept it from him that he'd lost close to $15,000 in that second robbery. I already knew he must be in a bad spot, for our office hadn't dared insure that second shipment.

I was a bit backward mentioning Tom Bemis and tackling the question of her feelings for him. She saw right through me and had this to say: "You must have gathered that he's asked me to marry him. Well, maybe I will. He's a fine man in a lot of ways."

"Then why not let him run things for you until your father's up and about?"

She gave me a queer look, one that was trying to see deep into me. "Would you wish your troubles onto a friend, Slim?"

It sounded good, her using the nickname I'd been known by ever since I got my first riding job. "No," I admitted, "I reckon I usually look out for myself."

"So do I. The quickest way to lose friends is to mix them into your private affairs."

"But you're going to marry him."

"Am I?" She gave me a funny sort of smile. "I wonder. Did you ever have this happen to you, Slim? You think a lot of a person who's really nice to you, gentlemanly and all, yet. . . ."

I waited a moment before asking: "Yet what?"

She turned away then, and went to the stove to lift the lid of the coffee pot to see if the water had come to a boil. Pretty soon she said: "Women must be exactly as contrary as they say. I honestly don't know what it is about Tom that doesn't satisfy me."

"He's a big man any way you look at him."

She nodded. "Yes."

That didn't tell me a thing. Nor did it give me any grounds for saying anything more about Bemis. So I switched to something else, telling her about Ed and how I'd found him.

She was plenty cut up about him, and asked what he'd looked like. I'd hardly said ten words before she interrupted with: "Why, I know that man. He was in Tom's office a week ago when I was up there. Wasn't he working for the Sunbeam?"

"He could've been. Or he and Bemis might have fixed it so it'd look like he was. What else do you know about him?"

Nothing, it turned out. She'd recognized him by the red shirt and his guns. But when it came to giving me a lead on how or why he'd been murdered, she was no help.

We had our coffee then, along with some cold biscuits and jam she took out of a cupboard, and by the time I was finished I felt more like going down to town and crawling into my blankets than doing what I had in mind. But I was being paid well for this job and something besides pay was pushing me along now, so as I finished the second cup I told her: "The quicker we get at this thing, the sooner we untangle it. I'd like to have a try at taking some of that gold out tonight."

"Tonight?" She looked like she couldn't believe what she was hearing.

"Sure, why not? You and I are the only ones that know who I am so far. And if you're going to throw lead at me, I might as well know it now."

That jolted her. "You can't be serious."

"In this sort of work you don't trust anyone, miss."

She took that like a man. "No, I don't suppose you can. But. . . ."

"But what?"

"I . . . well, I've just always thought Tom would advise me on this."

I lifted my shoulders. "If Tom knows about it, there's just one more chance of somebody saying something they shouldn't. Letting the cat out of the bag."

"Oh, he'd never betray a confidence like that!"

"I don't aim to give him the chance to. Not yet, that is. If I can haul out what gold you've got, then there'll be plenty of time to haul his."

I was leaving it plainly up to her. There were, after all, plenty of reasons why she shouldn't trust me. For one, I was a stranger. For another, I could have come by that Wells Fargo card in any number of ways. By taking it off Ed's body, for instance. Or by plain swiping it from someone's pocket.

Yet she never for a second questioned who I was. Sometimes it happens that way. Two people meet and, knowing not one blamed thing about the past, get along like old friends, trust each other all the way. It was that way from the beginning with Ruth Vance and me.

She asked: "You want the gold now?" And when I nodded, she said—"Just a minute."—and left the kitchen.

In a minute she was back with her hair gathered at the back of her neck with some sort of clasp, her coat on, and carrying a lantern. She looked kind of excited and, going to the kitchen door, told me: "You'll have to come along and help."

Outside, I followed her on up a path that shortly climbed the base of a muck dump and brought us to a tunnel mouth in the side of the cañon. Only after we'd stumbled a good ways in along the tunnel did she hand me the lantern and say: "No one can see us now."

I lit it, and we went farther on back until pretty soon she said—"This way."—and headed into a drift that took off from the main one.

We hadn't gone twenty yards along before we had to climb over a muck heap and some shoring timbers, lying strewn every which way. I could see the drift had long ago been abandoned. She was finally on her hands and knees, her head almost touching the rock overhead as she crawled over the rubble. Then she called—"I'll have to go the rest of the way. You're too big."—and she reached back a hand for the lantern.

Kneeling there, I looked over the top of the rock heap and saw her worm her way into a space beyond where there was a little more room. She lifted away some big hunks of rock. Then she began handing me these small, heavy buckskin sacks.

There were twelve of them and I was opening one as she crawled back and sat down beside me, setting the lantern aside.

As I sifted some of the yellow stuff into my palm, she told me: "Wire gold. If we can ever get it out, Dad can bring in machinery. From then on he's going to be living one of his dreams. Not of having money but of having made a big strike."

I hefted the sack and looked at the others. "How much would you say is here?"

"Nearly twenty thousand."

I whistled. Then, for a reason I'll never understand, I moved six of the sacks away from the other six. "This first try we'll take out only half."

"Why, Slim?"

"In case I don't make it."

"But you're going to!"

I shook my head, still not understanding that quirk in my thinking that was warning me against doing as she wanted. "Nope. I can always make another trip. No use gambling everything on one turn of the cards."

She agreed reluctantly, and I had her crawl on back and cache those extra six sacks where she'd got them. By the time she was with me again, I'd stuffed four I was taking into my pockets and, carrying the other two in my hands, we started picking our way over the litter toward the main tunnel.

We were talking—something about how I'd have to find a better horse, as I remember—and she was close alongside me, when we came out of the head of the drift. My back was to her, turning as I was into the main tunnel when suddenly she gave a cry.

There was a crash of breaking glass and the lantern went out. I dropped the gold sacks in my hands and reached down for the Colt. In the next half a second I sensed someone moving in on me—his boots made a scraping noise, I caught a whiff of his breath, stale with cigar smoke. Then half a million pinwheels and shooting stars blazed out across my eyes as something smashed like a mule kick at the side of my head. There wasn't much pain then, just a sort of crunch that seemed to shorten my backbone a good inch.

IV

The next thing I knew I was staring up at the light of a lantern and it hurt my eyes. Ruth and Matt White were standing there, looking down at me. I could catch the smell of coal oil strong in the air, and as my head rocked around I saw another lantern— the one Ruth had been carrying—lying all busted and on its side nearby on the rocky floor. My head felt like it was half full of loose jagged buckshot rolling around and tearing up the insides.

Ruth must have seen me open my eyes, because she came to her knees alongside me, saying real gentle: "Oh, Slim. We thought you were. . . ." She didn't say it, but I knew what she'd been thinking as she asked in that same tender way: "Can you talk?"

"I can if you'll hold onto the top of my skull," I told her.

Matt White looked worried and pretty quick he came down onto his knees right beside her, speaking like he was real sorry for me: "Just lay there till you feel like moving, friend. That was one hell of a close thing."

So I closed my eyes, drawing a breath slowly, wondering if it was the hangover from when I'd been hit that made me still smell that stale tobacco smoke. I had to know, so I rolled my head around and said: "White, take a good look here above my ear. See any busted bone?"

He leaned over close and took his look. And a second after he said: "The skin ain't even broke open, Slim. The hat must've took the crack." I caught that stale smell real strong.

Well, I closed my eyes again to stall for time, trying to fit Matt White into the puzzle. Then I remembered the gold and reached down and felt of the pockets of my waist overalls. They still bulged. I pushed up onto an elbow and looked out across the uneven rock floor, asking: "What about the sacks of stuff I was carrying?"

"He didn't get any of it, according to Miss Ruth," White said. Talk about your pokerfaces, he had one. Not by the bat of an eyelash did he let on he was anything but happy over the way things had turned out.

I sat up as best I could and pulled the four other buckskin pouches from my pockets. Handing them to Ruth, I said: "Better hide these where they were. I couldn't carry a feather duster from here to your cabin."

"I'm so sorry, Slim," she said as she took the sacks. "Matt, can you help him get to his feet? This won't take me long."

As she got up, she reached for the lantern, having a hard time of it because the sacks were so heavy and wanted to spill out of her arms.

Right after she walked away, leaving us in darkness, Matt took a hold of me and helped me stand. I was feeling a lot better even for the aching head; but made out I was pretty weak and groggy. We thrashed around there in the dark, me swaying from one side to the other and Matt holding on, trying to steady me, and all the while he was breathing sort of hard, giving me added proof that it was a whiff of his breath I had caught before I was knocked cold.

I didn't want to have to bed down with Matt during the night, so after he and Ruth had got me outside into the air and headed for the cabins, I bogged down as best I could and was finally relieved when she said: "It's nonsense to try to get him any farther, Matt. Put him in my bed and I'll use the couch in the other room."

So between them they half carried, half walked me into her cabin and into that bedroom where I could see her old man lying on the second bed. I complained in whispers about Matt trying to do more than pull off my boots, and as I sank back onto the mattress, old Vance stirred and called out in his sleep. Ruth put a finger to his lips and motioned Matt on out of the crowded room. As he tiptoed to the door, I closed my eyes and breathed real heavy, like I was already asleep.

For a couple of minutes after the door closed, I heard Matt and Ruth talking in low tones in the other room. Then the hinges of the outside door squealed a little and I heard the door softly close.

Before Matt White could have taken five strides, I was out of bed and pulling on my boots. I waited a few seconds at the bedroom door, listening. Then I inched it open to find the front room already dark.

"Miss Ruth," I whispered.

"Slim," came her hushed, startled answer.

I knew she must have been getting ready for bed, so after I'd come through the door and closed it, I stayed where I was to say: "I'm all right. Now listen to what I have to say. I'm going outside, leaving by way of the kitchen. You're to turn in and get some sleep and let on like I'm still in there with your father."

I heard her coming across toward me and a moment later she asked softly, that edge of excitement still in her words: "What is it, Slim? What are you doing? Can you walk by yourself?"

"Everything's all right. But there's something I've got to do."

"What, Slim?"

"Listen," I said. "You're going to have to trust me and not ask questions. But I've got to be out there to see something."

For a second or two she didn't say anything. Then: "Are you thinking he may still be in the tunnel, whoever it was?"

That gave me an out, so I told her: "You guessed it."

"But . . . but I heard him running out of the tunnel. I followed him, calling for Matt. He isn't in there, Slim. Unless he's gone back in since we came out."

"Maybe he has. By the way, how long was it before Matt showed up when you called him?"

"Right away."

"Did you get a look at this other one, the one that slugged me?"

"No. He pushed me and I fell. I was so frightened I tried to do something for you before I thought to call Matt. Then it was too late to see who it was."

I heaved a long sigh but then remembered it wouldn't have mattered much whatever she had seen or heard. She cut in on my thinking right then by coming up to me and laying a hand on my arm, asking: "You were pretending, Slim?"

"How do you mean?" She'd caught me off guard.

"To be feeling so bad?"

I couldn't help but laugh a little. "Maybe I was."

"Then you don't trust Matt?" she wanted to know, real quick.

"Did I say that?"

"No, but you're acting like you don't. What is it you know, Slim?"

Should I tell her or shouldn't I? Would she be able to keep from acting any different toward Matt White until this thing was settled? I was whipsawed, trying to make up my mind. But this girl had done something to me.

Maybe it was because she was standing so near, near enough so I could catch the fragrance of her hair, or maybe because she was trusting me, counting on me, that I finally broke down and told her what I knew—or, rather, what I'd decided.

She listened all the way without once butting in. And it was only when I'd finished that she asked in a lost voice: "But how could he be the one? Tom's known him for years. When we needed a man we could trust, Tom let Dad have him. He's worked hard for us."

"Gold's ruined many a good man, Ruth."

"But I can't believe it of Matt."

"You don't have to. Just act like you always do toward him and we'll see what happens."

"But what can you do? Now, tonight?"

"Maybe nothing. But I want to prowl around anyway."

She let me go finally and I left the cabin by the kitchen door, remembering the thicket of scrub oak growing close out back. I didn't really know what I was looking for but anyway worked over to the tunnel mouth without once showing myself, keeping to the trees and, closer in, hugging the shadows along the side of the cañon.

Before I went into the tunnel, I took off my boots, hid them, and drew the .45. Not that either would have done me much good if Matt White was waiting inside for me. But I couldn't see why he would be waiting. I'd put on a pretty fair act about feeling so bad and he'd have no reason for suspecting I'd be up and about.

It turned out that he wasn't waiting. But he was in that mine. My socks had gone cold and clammy within ten steps, and that uneven rock floor was bruising my feet so badly I wanted to turn back. But I kept on, now and then slamming into the side of the tunnel where it made a bend.

I'd have gone right on past that abandoned drift where the gold was hidden if it hadn't been for the lantern, just the faint glow of it. Sure enough he was in there.

I cat-footed close enough to the rubble heap to see him up there on top, throwing aside big chunks of rock. He knew the gold was there, he had all night to find it, and, regardless of how good Ruth had cached it, he'd run onto it in the end.

I could have killed him then easy as shooting a sitting sage hen with a double-barreled shotgun. But I didn't. Matt White was only a part of this thing, and maybe not such a big part.

Someone bigger was behind it, someone who could have hired enough men to handle those guards on that second shipment. I'd been sent in here to put an end to this. Killing Matt White wouldn't put an end to it. So I decided to use him.

I backed quietly out of the drift and walked maybe twenty strides toward the mouth of the main tunnel. Then I sat down and began to wait.

It was hard staying awake. It was hard to put down my appetite for tobacco and not roll up a smoke. The minutes dragged. But I stayed awake and in the end, after maybe a full hour, light suddenly wavered in the mouth of that drift.

I came to a stand and took out that Colt again. But I might've saved myself the trouble. For Matt White, his pockets bulging and other sacks cradled in the bend of his left arm, turned out of that drift and deeper into the tunnel.

So he *wasn't* taking the gold out. That relieved me a lot. There wasn't much more to be done now but make sure of him. So I eased on out of the tunnel, pulled my boots back on, and, sure enough, in about ten more minutes out he came. He wasn't carrying anything but the lantern.

I watched him sneak away, being just as careful about not showing himself as I'd been coming in. I let him get a ten-minute start on me before I headed for the Vance cabin the way I'd come, out of sight and hoping Ruth was asleep.

She wasn't.

She heard me come in and right away began asking questions. How come I'd been away so long? Had I seen anyone?

Now there are things you can't tell a woman. Not that you can't trust females, but there are just some things a man can handle better alone. This double-crossing of Matt White's was that sort of thing. If she knew about him, I ran the chance of her giving it away, scaring him off. And I was counting on Matt

184

as the bird dog that would lead me to the big augur, whoever he was.

So I lied like hell, telling her I'd been roaming through the diggings and hadn't found hide nor hair of anyone.

The last thing she said before I made her go in to her own bed was: "Slim, it's like I've known you a long time and can wish all my troubles onto you. Things will come out all right, won't they?"

"Don't you worry for a minute," I told her before I closed the bedroom door and heard her lock it from the inside.

As I dropped off to sleep on the couch, the ache nearly gone from my head, I was wishing I could believe in my own medicine.

V

Ruth woke me next morning and took me in and made me acquainted with her father. The old man was worried when he heard what had happened to me last night—how could we keep it from him?—and I got out of there as quickly as I could without hurting his feelings.

You could see he was something of a man, even though his face was drawn and hollow-cheeked from the fever and pain he'd had. He had the same fine features as Ruth and, though his hair was almost all gray, it had been the same color as hers. She must have got her eyes from her mother, for his were a warm brown.

Matt White came over and ate breakfast in the kitchen with me, and I did a good job of buttering him up. Over by the tunnel I could now and then hear sounds, and after the meal was finished, I stepped out back to see several men wheeling barrows of muck on out of the tunnel and dumping them down the heap. Pretty soon Matt went up there to boss things and Ruth and I had a chance to talk.

I was going over to the Sunbeam, I told her, and see Tom Bemis. What was I going to tell him? I didn't know yet. But if she
met Bemis before I had a chance to see her again, she wasn't to
let on about last night unless he began talking about it.

She didn't ask me why I might not tell Bemis about last night.
Which was one more proof to me that she was trusting me
plenty. And darned if I thought that card of Wells Fargo's had
everything to do with her acting that way. She just believed in
me, Wells Fargo or no.

It's a sin and a shame for a man to mistreat a horse and
you'll have to take my word for it when I say I'd forgotten about
that hired gray tied down in the timber. I was cussing myself for
a knothead as I walked down to him. But he was just as I had
left him, no worse for a night out. And it was just as hard to
make him go down that trail as it had been to push him up it.

On the way across to the Sunbeam I began wondering why
Matt hadn't had more questions to ask about how I happened
to be in the mine with Ruth last night. Especially after I'd
pretended to turn down the job.

I didn't know how Ruth might have explained it to him. But
here was just one more item to chalk up against his crooked-
ness. When a shady character runs onto something he doesn't
understand, he figures he can't afford to ask too many questions. Matt certainly hadn't asked too many.

Bemis was in his office. I got in the gate after I'd given the
guard my name and he had called across that Slim wanted to
see the boss. Once I was in there, sitting across the desk from
Bemis, I got straight down to cases and told him about last
night—everything but about me being on Wells Fargo's payroll
and about what I'd seen Matt doing later. When he asked why
I'd gone back to see the girl after refusing the job, I gave him an
honest answer.

"Figured I'd stand more of a chance taking that gold out if

just I and she knew I was doing it." Then, to make it sound more convincing, I stretched the truth some. "Mister, I need that hundred bucks. And I'll be needing it pretty soon."

But he was only half listening and sat there frowning like he was trying to think. All of a sudden he looked across at me and asked: "What about Matt White?"

"What about him?" I was innocent as the preacher's wife.

"Could it have been him that slugged you?"

I let my mouth hang open. "How could it? Miss Vance ran and called him out of his bunk."

"Still, it could have been him. You said whoever did it ran out of the tunnel."

"Hell, don't we have to trust someone in this?" I came back at him. "Matt looks honest to me."

"So he does," Bemis admitted. He seemed relieved I was convinced of Matt's honesty. He sighed then, saying: "Well, it beats me. But someone's sure put the Indian sign on Vance. And on me."

"I've been thinking the thing over," I told him. "Now, suppose Matt and me made a try at it together. Like this. You give us each enough of your gold to put in the pouches on our hulls. Not a big load anyone could spot easy, understand. Just enough to hide away like it was the grub and possibles we'd naturally be carrying. He and I could mosey on out that trail come dark tonight. And ten to one we'd make it without even being stopped."

He looked at me kind of queer for a second, I thought. But then I couldn't be sure about the look as he gave a nod.

"Why not? You could carry several thousand that way. And if you made it this time, you could do it again. You'd have to be damn' careful of that trail down the rim. I might even talk it around that you're taking out plans to some engineer in Granite City to check about machinery we've ordered."

"Sure, you could cook up some story."

He went serious. "Of course I'd want to try it with Vance's gold. Because it looks like we have a good chance. His credit's poor outside on account of this. He can't even buy grub for his crew. Maybe you noticed he doesn't have an eat shack. There used to be one, but when his credit played out, they tore it down and used the timber in the mine."

"You can't be in such good shape yourself."

"Forget me," he said, and I'll admit I admired that kind of talk. "I'll scrape through somehow till we're over this trouble. It's different with Fred Vance. He's had nothing but bad luck. Then there's Ruth."

I suppose it was mention of Ruth that made me do what I did just then. Sure, she was his and maybe I envied him because he was her chosen man. But he was trying to help her the same as I was, and that's what decided me to say: "There's one thing I haven't told you, Bemis. I'm the Wells Fargo man you've been expecting."

He reared back in his chair, surprised as all get out. His face took on a blank look pretty quickly after that and he drawled: "I hope you can prove it. Because, if you can, you and I are going to blow this thing wide open. Between us we'll collect some scalps."

I took out my wallet and showed him the card and then, to convince him further, told him about Ed. That seemed to sober him more than anything and afterward, when he handed back the card, he said: "So his name was Demmler? Maybe you know I'd hired him. He was using another handle, Ed Spane. Now I find out you're Spane."

I nodded, too busy thinking of something else to say anything else. For it came to me then that if Ed in his playful way had used my name, and if the handle had had anything to do with his winding up where he was now, then whoever had killed him might have thought they were doing away with me.

Every now and then a man gets a jolt like that, something that brings him wide-awake to danger. I told myself: *Keep on talking and you'll wind up with a wood nightshirt, Spane.*

That was why I didn't spill the rest to Tom Bemis, though I'd been on the verge of it—about Matt White and how the gold had been moved.

We went on from there, Bemis and I, planning how he'd get good horses for me and Matt and come up to the President Grant right after dark. He gave me the name of the banker in Granite City we'd turn the gold over to when—and if—we got through.

And as I left him, he told me: "Keep an eye on Matt, Spane. I've trusted him like a brother until now. Maybe he's all right. But watch him."

Leaving the Sunbeam, I went on down to town and loafed around, just killing time. Had my hair trimmed and got a shave and watched the animals, mostly mules, going up and down the street. It wasn't hard to imagine what a boom camp Lode would soon be, for one string of animals coming up the cañon was loaded with machinery parts and what looked like pieces for an ore wagon. They'd haul a whole stamp mill and maybe even a smelter up that narrow trail in the end, crazy as they were over the yellow stuff. There was already a sawmill set up below town and so many new buildings and shacks you could hardly count them.

Along about 4:00 I threw the saddle on the roan at the corral and moseyed on up to the President Grant. Ruth was cleaning house, had all the furniture moved out front, and I got right to work helping her, hardly thinking it wasn't a man's place to be housecleaning. She didn't belittle me by asking me to sweep or polish windows or any woman's work like that, but let me do the moving of the heavy pieces and such.

All the while her father and I were talking back and forth, and when I told the plans for the evening, I talked to both him and Ruth. They were both on edge and I did all I could to calm them down, and when Matt showed up for supper, we had to go all over it again. They pitched in and helped me persuade him it wouldn't be too risky.

He talked against it, of course—knowing what was bound to happen when we went to get the gold—but he could go only so far and in the end had to agree it was a good scheme.

When we were finishing supper, I said: "Ruth, we might as well go up there and bring down those sacks now. It'll be dark in another half hour and Bemis'll be here with the horses."

She got up from the table and, when I left my chair, she looked at Matt and said: "You might as well be the one to help me, Matt. Just for the fun of it, I'd like you to know where I've kept those sacks hidden."

That got me real panicked and I tried to think of something to say to keep Matt from going with her. But what could I say that wouldn't have given it away I didn't trust him? It helped a little to realize he wasn't going to harm her, for he'd have no reason, so I finally watched them take a lantern and leave, feeling nervous as all get out.

They hadn't been gone ten minutes when I heard her call from up by the tunnel mouth. I was looking out into the dusk, seeing her running for the cabin, Matt following more slowly, when I heard the stomp of horses out front and realized it must be Tom Bemis.

Talk about not knowing whether you're coming or going, none of us did for the next few minutes. The most important thing that came out of those minutes was that Ruth, in telling how the gold wasn't there, was talking to me and not to Bemis, even though he was standing there with us by the back door.

Ruth was fit to be tied. She looked like maybe the mine had

caved in or someone had been hurt real bad. She was stunned, couldn't believe it.

I noticed how Tom Bemis kept watching Matt, and pretty soon he asked: "Know anything about this mess at all, Matt?"

"Not a blessed thing, Tom. Unless this jasper that belted Slim came back afterward and spent the night digging in that drift. She had it hid in a good spot. That much I do know."

Ruth finally looked at Bemis. When all the talk had started, she'd closed the kitchen door, warning us not to speak too loud for fear her father would get wind of what had happened. And now she said to Bemis: "What's going to happen to us? To Dad? This may do him more harm than anything has."

Tom Bemis showed he was something of a man right then when he stepped over to her, put an arm around her shoulder, and drew her close to him. It was as kindly a gesture almost as I've ever seen.

What he said was: "From now on we're throwing our luck together, Ruth. You and your dad and I. This time I won't take no for an answer."

That hit her hard and to hide the tears that were brimming in her eyes, she turned and buried her face against his shoulder. He patted her on the back, saying in a gentle way: "Spane's told you who he is, Ruth, a Wells Fargo man. He's thought up a good way of getting our gold out. Just don't worry. A month from now, after we've opened that new drift through from the Sunbeam and joined it to your tunnel, we'll be taking so much out of this hill, we'll never miss what's been stolen. We're going to rename the outfit the Ruth. We'll build a fine house up there along that point and your dad'll come there to live with us. Now just let on like this hasn't happened."

She was dabbing at her eyes with a handkerchief, and when she finally looked up at Bemis, she was trying to smile. "You're so good, Tom. So downright generous that I. . . ."

"If I'm half good enough for you, nothing else matters," Bemis said.

I couldn't stick around and watch any longer, so I eased on past the corner of the cabin and Matt followed me.

"This is the damnedest thing I ever run onto," he said as he rolled up a smoke. Passing the makings to me, he added: "Well, them two have been a long time getting together. So maybe it's for the best this happened. They'll make a fine couple."

"Which don't cut any ice on what I was sent here to do." I didn't intend to sound sour, but I was surely feeling just that.

"So you're a Wells Fargo gunhand," he said. "Danged if you didn't have me fooled with all that talk about needing a hundred so bad."

"Maybe I will be needing it. Maybe I'll be out of a job if I can't untangle this mess."

He looked at me, real serious. "You really think we ought to go ahead and make that try tonight?"

"What with?"

It was Tom Bemis who answered that. A second or two ago I'd heard the kitchen door close and now Bemis came walking up to us. The first thing he said was: "You two are going on down to Granite City just the same. Right now. I got to thinking it wasn't right, Vance taking the whole risk. So I brought along a shipment from the Sunbeam. You can divvy it up between you and go along just the same as though this hadn't happened."

Matt gave him a puzzled look, or so I thought, although the look didn't tell me anything. He said—"Anything you say, Tom."—and led the way over to the three horses tied to the rail in front of his cabin. By now it was nearly dark.

They were fine animals, all three, mine a black with two white front stockings. I had to let out the stirrups because I'm so long-jointed, while Matt had to take up his. Meantime, Bemis was taking some small canvas sacks from the bags on his saddle and dividing them between Matt and me.

We'd been working in poor light and by the time we were ready to ride it was plenty dark.

Bemis said: "The moon'll be up in a few more minutes now. Forget how light it'll be and head straight down the trail like you had nothing but time and didn't care who saw you. Do you have those invoices, Matt?"

"What invoices?"

"Didn't I tell you about it? Kramer's been billing Vance for that assay outfit for three months now. I want you to take down the invoices and pay him."

Matt dropped the reins and went on up to his cabin. While I was tightening my cinch, Bemis sauntered on up there and met him. They passed a few words I didn't catch and I saw Bemis take the sheets of paper Matt had brought out and look at them. Then Bemis handed them back and they came on down, and Matt and I climbed into our hulls.

"We're counting on you, Spane . . . Ruth and I," Bemis said as we went away.

I just lifted a hand to him and kept right on, Matt close behind me, and neither of us spoke till we were down off the slope and the town was in sight below. Then Matt said: "We're sure as hell taking a chance."

"Not such a big one," I told him. "Who could know about it besides you and me, the girl, her old man, and Bemis? The reason they got stopped those other times was because the whole town knew the gold was going out."

We went on down and through the town and, believe you me, the lid was off the place with the saloons crowded and more drunks than I'd ever seen in such a short stretch.

"Pay night," Matt told me once when he had to rein aside and out of the way of a man staggering across the street. We watched this jasper try and wade the creek and not quite make it. He fell flat on his face just short of the far bank, and some gents who'd been watching him whooped and hollered but didn't offer to help him get on his feet.

Pretty soon the town was behind us and we were riding the trail through the timber. The moon was up with its light sifting in between the trees. Matt was still behind me and, when we hit the spots where it was really dark, a chill ran up and down my backbone and I was plenty worried.

Then all of a sudden, along one of those dark patches, he said: "What the hell's wrong with this mare? She's limping."

"Better get down and have a look." I stopped and turned, so as to be facing him. He couldn't see it but my right hand was wrapped tightly around the handle of my Colt.

When he was aground, the fussing with one of his mare's back hoofs, I finally let go of the .45. After a couple minutes he said: "Damned rock. How's the blade on your knife?"

"Plenty stout." I took out my clasp knife and handed it down to him, and he got to work again, now and then cussing the mare for not standing steady.

It was taking him a long time, so I rolled up a smoke and lit it, watching him all the while and also looking off through the trees. Then after a few minutes I heard a sound from out there toward the south slope, like someone or some animal moving through the underbrush.

That quick I decided Matt's mare had no more had a rock caught in her shoe than I had one in mine. I dropped my smoke, pulled the .45, and dismounted.

"There," Matt said as I walked in on him. "That got it." He dropped her hoof, snapped the blade of the knife shut, and reached out to hand it to me, looking at me for the first time.

He went stiff as a poker when he saw my hardware lined at him. He dropped the knife and lifted his hands alongside his

194

shoulders. "What the hell, Spane?"

Before I told him what, I picked up the knife and dropped it in my pocket. Then I took off my hat and held it out to him. "Let's have yours," I said.

Mine was wider than his, a light gray with a curled brim. His was black with a flat brim. He didn't say anything as he took mine, then handed me his.

"Try it on for size, Matt."

He did. I knew it fit him because his fit me fair enough. And now, listening real hard, I found that the sounds off near the slope had died out. Whatever had been making them I wasn't sure of but could guess.

"Now the coat," I told him. "And move real slow, fella."

So we traded coats. His was some too small for me and my faded blue jumper was big for him, but when the light's not too good such points aren't noticeable.

Only when I walked in behind him and lifted the .38 from the scabbard he wore high at his belt did he begin complaining. "Mind telling me what kind of a game this is?" he asked.

"Not at all, Matt. Y'see, I was in the tunnel last night and saw you digging for those sacks. You want to tell me now who you're working for or do I have to turn you over to the law in Granite City and let you think it over?"

I'd seen him stiffen when I mentioned last night. But he got his nerve back in a hurry and now all he said was: "Spane, you're off your head."

"Maybe so." I shucked the shells out of his Colt and gave it to him again. "Just put that back where it came from, Matt. Then we'll change hulls."

I made him do it all on his own and with the gold those saddles were real heavy and he grunted as he worked. But finally his saddle was on the black and mine on his mare, with one of the blankets folded and him sitting on it when he climbed the black, looking higher than he really was.

This would have to do, I decided. And as I climbed into leather, behind him now, I said: "Matt, I ought to warn you about me knowing a trick or two with a handgun. Sometime I'll show you. Lately I've been practicing on a sardine can. You know, heaving it up, drawing, and then seeing how many times I can hit it before it touches the ground. Most times it's four. Sometimes I can even get that fifth hunk of lead into it."

He snorted something I couldn't make out, and I told him: "Now go along real easy, like we had plenty of time."

He did go on, for about three hundred yards. Then he pulled in and turned around and there was a sort of whine in his throat as he said: "Listen, Spane, I. . . ."

"You what?"

"I'll split that gold with you."

"Brother, you've seen the last of that gold. But you could tell me where you hid it."

"All right. It's under that windlass they used to haul muck up with out of the glory hole. Now you going to let me go?"

"Nope."

He used some pretty salty words on me then, and I let him go right ahead, afterward hefting the Colt out again and saying: "On second thought, mister, I'll hold this in my lap. If you decide you'd rather take your chances with it than whatever you had cooked up for me, make a run for it."

"What did I have cooked up for you?"

"That's what we're going to find out. Or I should say, *you* are. You look like me, you're forking my jughead. Now get moving and we'll find out."

He didn't, not until I drew the hammer back and he heard the .45 click. And when he did go on, we hadn't ridden more than fifty yards before we rounded a bend and there, ahead of us and standing out by itself away from the trees, lay the ruined cabin where I'd found Ed.

He slowed just then and I knew for sure the cabin was to be the spot where they'd counted on hailing me. I said—"Keep going, friend."—and he rode on. Pretty soon he started swinging wide of the trail, away from the cabin.

I decided to let him go and just followed on behind him, watching both him and the cabin now.

We were almost even with it when, quick as a flash, he yelled and doubled over in the saddle, reining the black to one side and digging in the spurs. You couldn't have told it was his voice. Neither could the other man, the one in the cabin.

I saw a spurt of red flame lick out from one of the empty black windows. I saw Matt White jerk sideways like he'd brushed against a tree trunk. The black shied in its hard run and Matt was pitched out of his hull, and I'd guess he somersaulted three or four times before he wound up sprawled out against a boulder.

A couple of other things had happened during that second or two. First, the blanket had left the saddle with Matt so you couldn't miss it. Next, you could see as he fell he wasn't nearly so tall as he'd looked sitting on his hull, as I'd have been.

So I yanked the mare on around and made tracks back for the timber and I didn't hear the rifle when it was let off at me, only felt a puff of air alongside my cheek.

Once in the trees I pulled in and turned around. Sure enough, out from the back of the cabin cut a horse and rider.

Oh, he was safe enough all right. I didn't have a Winchester on the saddle or he'd have been dead right then. Watching him go away, finally running his horse straight out down the trail, my hands were itching for a .30-30.

I waited till I could barely hear him ahead of me before I cut out after him, not pushing the mare very fast at that. Passing where Matt was lying, I thought about stopping. But there wasn't too much time and anyway I knew it was no use.

Down below where the pines closed once more, I left the trail and rode the creek, making time as best I could. It didn't take long to bring the sound of the falls within hearing, and, knowing I was close to the rim, I cut back to the trail again.

Just short of it I stopped and left the mare, and went on afoot, being plenty careful. Finally I could see the trail. There wasn't anyone on it, so I edged on over to the rim and went belly down, looking over.

You could see all of the first quarter mile of the trail snaking off to the north before the overhangs blocked the view. It was empty. A sort of a panic hit me then, thinking this killer had outguessed me. Then I caught a sound from below, a sharp one like maybe an iron shoe hitting a rock.

So my hopes bounced back up again. I crossed the trail and walked on along the rim till I came to a heap of boulders. They were heavier than they looked. The one I rolled over the rim's edge didn't reach much higher than my knee.

But it was enough to turn the trick. I've never been so damned scared. You could hear the boulder bang off a ledge below, then more rock start falling. Then there came this roar, and I felt the ground shaking under me. I ran as hard as I could, getting out of there.

After it was over, I walked back and chanced another peek downward. It looked pretty much the same, this upper end of the trail undamaged. But I knew it couldn't be the same below. No one would be using the rim trail for some time to come.

Now came the ticklish part. I settled down to wait. A pine seedling taller than I was grew close to the head of the trail, and I stood behind that. You can bet your life I had the Colt in my hand. The time for taking chances was over.

Had he gone down with the rock slide or was he still alive? The longer the minutes dragged out, the more I thought the first guess might be the right one. Rock kept breaking away down there and setting up quite a racket.

The explosion came from behind me, so sudden and unexpected it caught me with the .45 hanging at my side. It and the branch breaking off in front of my face came at the same time. I wheeled around, thinking he must have climbed straight up the rim from near the head of the trail, knowing I'd be waiting for him. How long he'd been looking before he spotted me is anyone's guess.

You think out what you'd do times like that and you don't do them. This jolt against my shoulder rocked me back. I'd caught the wink of his gun, then could see him crouched by the edge of the rim. I hefted the Colt up and lined it and didn't count my shots, didn't quit till the hammer clicked on an empty.

I saw him rear up, lose balance, and fall backward. The length of time it took for the sound of his landing to reach me from below told me him and Matt were together now the same as they'd been all along.

You know who he was as well as I did. But I wanted to make sure. My shoulder didn't really begin hurting till I'd walked down there and found him hanging over the edge of the trail. Tom Bemis.

That was his way of making love, I reckon, stealing his own and the Vance gold so Ruth would have to get hitched with him. He was after something else, too, for a couple months later we worked a drift of the President Grant on across in the direction of the Sunbeam and struck the biggest paying vein they ever worked in the Lode field. He must have been geologist enough to have guessed where that vein would be. Marrying Ruth would have got it for him.

Lode grew fast as a lamb, but a lot wilder. Instead of just fixing that quarter mile of trail I'd caved in while getting Bemis, they blasted out a real road, taking months to do it. Then the freight wagons poured in and buildings went up, one of them a church. Ruth and I were the parson's first paying customers.

ABOUT THE AUTHOR

Peter Dawson is the *nom de plume* used by Jonathan Hurff Glidden. He was born in Kewanee, Illinois, and was graduated from the University of Illinois with a degree in English literature. In his career as a Western writer he published sixteen Western novels and wrote over 120 Western short novels and short stories for the magazine market. From the beginning he was a dedicated craftsman who revised and polished his fiction until it shone as a fine gem. His Peter Dawson novels are noted for their adept plotting, interesting and well-developed characters, their authentically researched historical backgrounds, and his stylistic flair. During the Second World War, Glidden served with the U.S. Strategic and Tactical Air Force in the United Kingdom. Later in 1950 he served for a time as Assistant to Chief of Station in Germany. After the war, his novels were frequently serialized in *The Saturday Evening Post*. Peter Dawson titles such as *Royal Gorge* and *Ruler of the Range* are generally conceded to be among his best titles, although he was an extremely consistent writer, and virtually all his fiction has retained its classic stature among readers of all generations. One of Jon Glidden's finest techniques was his ability, after the fashion of Dickens and Tolstoy, to tell his stories via a series of dramatic vignettes that focus on a wide assortment of different characters, all tending to develop their own lives, situations, and predicaments, while at the same time propelling the general plot of the story toward a suspenseful conclusion. He was no less gifted as a master of the short novel and short story. *Dark Riders of Doom* (Five Star Westerns, 1996) was the first collection of his Western short novels and stories to be published. Many Peter Dawson collections have followed in the Five Star Westerns.